Fic
Bou   Boutis, Victoria.
         Looking out

DATE DUE			
MAR. 1 1 1998			

GAYLORD M2

LOOKING OUT

VICTORIA BOUTIS

FOUR WINDS PRESS
New York

Lines from "Solidarity Forever" appear by permission of Alpha Music, Inc.

"Ma Curly Headed Baby" composed by George H. Clutsam
© 1897 by Edwin Ashdown Limited, 8/9 Frith Street,
London WIV 5TZ, England. Extract by permission.

"How Much is That Doggie in the Window" by Bob Merrill
© 1952 ® 1981 Golden Bell Songs (USA and Canada)
and Chappell Music Co. (worldwide except USA and Canada).
All rights reserved. Used by permission.

Lines from "My Loved One" were first published in Sing Out! magazine
Volume 3, Number 3, and appear with their kind permission.

Four Winds Press
Macmillan Publishing Company
866 Third Avenue, New York, NY 10022
Collier Macmillan Canada, Inc.
First Edition
Printed in the United States of America

10 9 8 7 6 5 4 3 2 1

The text of this book is set in 12 point Electra.

Library of Congress Cataloging-in-Publication Data
Boutis, Victoria.
Looking out / by Victoria Boutis.
p.   cm.
Summary: Though pleased to be part of the "in" crowd at her new
school, Ellen's growing awareness of her parents' social concerns,
expressed in their support of the condemned Rosenbergs, forces her
to make a choice about what really matters in life.
ISBN 0-02-711830-4
[1. Conduct of life—Fiction. 2. Parent and child—Fiction.
3. Responsibility—Fiction. 4. Schools—Fiction.] I. Title.
PZ7.B66876Lo 1988
[Fic]—dc19
87-36455   CIP   AC

For Florence and Joe

Ellen Gerson tucked a fourth salami sandwich into the brown paper bag. That made one for each member of the family.

"Let's get organized here," her father said. "Do you have the leaflets?" he asked her mother.

"Right here." Mrs. Gerson nodded toward a stack of papers cradled in one arm.

"Let's go, then. Everyone into the car," Mr. Gerson said.

"Ca, ca," Mikey echoed, holding up his arms. Ellen picked up her little brother and followed her parents out to the car. She settled Mikey in the backseat and sat down beside him.

The Gersons had only moved here to Fairmore Hills, Pennsylvania, two days before. Ellen's family had moved several times before, but the moves had always been from one apartment in one city to another apartment in another city. Their house in Fairmore Hills was very different—brand-new and with a patch of ground around it, still mostly dirt, with a few pale green shoots of new grass poking through.

1

As Mr. Gerson backed out of the driveway and started down the street, Ellen rested her chin on top of the front seat, midway between her parents. That way she could listen to their conversation and look out the front window at her new surroundings at the same time.

The car approached a trio of green plastic elves on a lawn. "Look at that, Mikey," Ellen said.

He stood up on the seat and waved at the statues.

At the next house, a man was bent over a long, cylindrical object, unrolling it across his front yard. "Look! A grass rug!" Ellen said, as the man's yard changed instantly from bare dirt to green lawn.

"Rass ruck," said Mikey.

Ellen laughed. "Okay, sit down now, Mikey," she told him.

"No," he asserted, with typical two-year-old defiance.

Ellen wrapped her arms around his legs and brought him to a sitting position. Then she turned back to her parents. Her mother's words were lost in Mikey's giggle behind her, but she heard her father say, "No, don't you see? They might try to ignore us, but eventually they'll have to listen."

Ellen turned around. Mikey was standing up again. "Come on, Mikey," she said, and pushed the back of his knees with one arm, forcing him down. He was up again almost immediately, laughing.

"Mom!" Ellen complained. "Mikey keeps standing up."

"Tell him to sit down," Mrs. Gerson said automatically over her shoulder.

Ellen clenched her teeth. She felt around in the brown paper bag and brought out a small box of raisins. "Here," she said, forcing Mikey down to a sitting position again and handing him the raisins. This time he settled back against the seat, and she sat forward, just in time to catch the end of her mother's reply.

". . . afraid we're just going through the motions now."

"Do you really believe that?" her father said. "In that case, I might as well turn around. We'll take the sandwiches and have a picnic." He glared at Mrs. Gerson, defying her to agree with him.

Ellen's mother stared back at him. Then she sighed—her sign of surrender. "No, you're right, Jess. Of course we have to go. I'm just so tired of it all. Running to Washington. Writing letters. Marching. What good have we done?"

Mr. Gerson stopped for a red light. He drummed his fingers on the steering wheel. Then he turned toward his wife. "Don't give up now," he said. "We need you." He reached across to her and tilted her chin up until their eyes met and she smiled into his.

"Hey, Dad, the light's green," Ellen said.

"Oh, yeah. Thanks, El," Mr. Gerson said. They lurched ahead.

Though Ellen had missed the first part of her parents' discussion, she was sure that they had been talking about the Rosenbergs, Julius and Ethel, who were in prison. The government had said that they were spies, that they had given the secret of the atom bomb to the Russians, and so they must die. But Ellen's parents had told her that they were innocent—good and decent people. The problem now was to convince everyone else—the judge, the jury, the FBI, the President—of the truth. That was why they were driving to New York City today: to join a protest march.

"How about a sandwich?" Mr. Gerson said now.

"Oh, Jess. Can't you wait? The sandwiches are for lunch," Mrs. Gerson said.

"Sorry," Mr. Gerson said, "but that smell is driving me crazy." He was silent for a while. Then he asked, "How about a half?"

"You're impossible," Mrs. Gerson said. She reached into the backseat, took half a sandwich from the lunch bag, and handed it to her husband. He took a hefty bite and breathed out a contented "mmmmmm."

Mrs. Gerson laughed. "If I could bottle a perfume called 'Essence of Garlic' you'd be the happiest man on earth."

"I'm getting hungry, too, Mom," Ellen said, as the garlicky smell of salami permeated the car. She helped herself to the other half of the sandwich, breaking off a section for Mikey. No one spoke for a while as Ellen, Mikey, and Mr. Gerson chewed. Mrs. Gerson sighed.

"I can't sit here and listen to you people eat." She reached back and took half a sandwich for herself.

Ellen looked out the window and read the billboards that flicked by. The words "You belong in a '53 Ford!" blazed above an illustration of a bright yellow car. Another sign pictured a woman whose hair was as sleek and yellow as the car's finish. "Soap dulls hair," the words above her read. "Halo glorifies it!"

Ellen scanned the road, searching for a Burma Shave sign: white with red letters. Was that one up ahead? Yes. The sign had one word: "Unless." A few moments later they reached a second white sign with red letters. "Your face," it said. Further ahead, a third sign added "Is stinger free." Then they drove past "You'd better let" and "Your honey be!" Finally, they reached the sign that ended every series: "Burma Shave!"

Ellen loved to read the chopped-up phrases of the Burma Shave rhymes. She grinned and recited this one back. "Unless your face is stinger free, you'd better let your honey be!"

Mr. Gerson threw a glance at Ellen. "Ah, the creative genius of the free enterprise system," he said.

"Don't tease, Jess," Mrs. Gerson said. She reached over and rubbed the back of her hand against her husband's cheek. "You could use a little Burma Shave yourself."

They were getting close to the city now. Ellen remembered the giant mushrooms of the oil tanks and the electric green color of the hills of waste chemicals from her last trip. In the hazy distance she could see the jagged outline of New York's skyscrapers. Now they were passing the roadside tire stands with their polished hubcaps nailed to trees and rough, hand-painted signs announcing TIRES * CHEAP * TIRES. All around were lopsided piles, columns, pyramids of tires.

"Okay, folks," Mr. Gerson said. "Lincoln Tunnel coming up."

Mikey scrambled up in his seat. "No! No leaky tunnel!" he cried, tears immediately springing to his eyes and sliding down his cheeks.

"Silly boy," Ellen said, laughing. "It's not a leaky tunnel. It's the *Lincoln* Tunnel." But she put her arm around her little brother and held him tight. Ellen wasn't worried about leaks, as Mikey was, but she always took a deep breath before their car burrowed underground. Tunnels made her nervous, too. Somehow, when she was much younger, she had begun to link tunnels with war. She didn't know why, but whenever she tried to imagine War—where Aunt Sonia's husband, her uncle Saul, had gone and never returned— she saw a tunnel. Inside her imaginary War tunnel, in an eerie, shadowless light, two groups of soldiers lined the narrow passage and shot at each other. Now, even though she knew that wars were fought in different ways—with tanks and planes and submarines, and bombs that dropped from the sky—it was a relief when they drove up toward the light.

When their car pulled out of the tunnel and into the city's narrow streets, Mrs. Gerson also breathed a contented sigh. "Ah, home," she said.

Ellen knew that, though her parents had left Manhattan four years before, they still considered themselves New Yorkers. "The City," as they called it, was

6

where their *real* friends were. Ellen had friends in New York, too—though they were mostly the children of her parents' friends. Still, in her memory, her days in New York were all happy ones.

Now Mr. Gerson maneuvered their car through the streets toward Fifth Avenue. "Look! Over there!" Ellen cried, and pointed toward a milling crowd.

"Yup," Mr. Gerson said. "They're our people." He parked the car on a side street and they hurried to join the throng.

Ellen hadn't ever seen so many people in one place like this before. There were lots of old people with wrinkled faces and white hair, lots of babies in carriages, and people of every age and size in-between. A couple of times, seeing a mass of dark curly hair above a brightly embroidered blouse, Ellen was on the verge of throwing her arms around her aunt Sonia, only to realize at the last moment that it wasn't Aunt Sonia after all.

The march had begun. People were moving up the avenue in straggly lines of eight or nine across. They didn't look much like the soldiers marching in file that Ellen had seen in movie newsreels. These people walked with ordinary, unmatched steps. But when Ellen looked behind her and could see no end to the flowing crowd, she felt a thrill at being one of them.

While Ellen and her family were waiting for their turn to join the march, a thin young man beside her asked, "Would you like to carry a sign?"

"Oh, yes!" Ellen said, feeling very grown-up. She looked at the signs in his pile. Some had pictures of

7

Julius and Ethel Rosenberg over the words "We Are Innocent." Others carried pictures of their two sons and the caption "Save Our Parents." Ellen pulled out one that said "Free Them!" in blue letters on a rectangle of white cardboard. She hoisted it to her shoulder.

"Jess! Mollie! How are you! Mikey! Oh, you cutie! And Ellen! How's my beautiful niece?" Suddenly Ellen was crushed against Aunt Sonia's chest. She tried to keep the sign free so it wouldn't get crushed, too. It was hard, though, not to get swept up in Aunt Sonia's enthusiasm. Ellen laughed and hugged her back. It was also nice to have someone call her beautiful—even if that someone was an aunt.

They began walking, Mr. Gerson on the left with Mikey on his shoulders, then Mrs. Gerson, then Ellen and her aunt Sonia on the outside. Behind her Ellen heard the beginnings of a song. The words carried like an electric spark from person to person until the singing ignited at the chorus.

> Hold the fort, for we are coming
> Union men be strong
> Side by side, we'll battle onward
> Victory will come!

Then, without a break, the thread of a new song wove through the marchers.

> When the union's inspiration through the
>   workers' blood shall run
> There can be no power greater anywhere
>   beneath the sun. . . .

Ellen knew all the words. As she sang, she thought back to the time Miss LoPresto, her fifth-grade music teacher, taught her class "John Brown's Body." Miss LoPresto had picked out the first notes on the piano and told the class the song would be easy to remember because it had the same tune as "Glory! Glory! Hallelujah." Ellen had never heard of "Glory! Glory! Hallelujah," but the tune was familiar. She knew it as "Solidarity Forever," the same song they were singing now. At the chorus she waved her sign in time to the music and sang as loud as she could.

Solidarity forever
Solidarity forever
Solidarity forever
The union makes us strong.

With the music swelling around her, Ellen did feel strong. Strong and happy. The feeling stayed with her through the next song, though this one was slow and mournful.

When Israel was in Egypt's land
Let my people go
Oppressed so hard
They could not stand
Let my people go.

Go down, Moses,
Way down in Egypt land
Tell old Pharaoh
Let my people go.

A barricade of wooden sawhorses formed a border along the marching route. There were policemen, some standing in groups of twos and threes, others on horses, at the edges of the barricades. Scattered groups of people stood behind this makeshift fence and stared at the marchers. A few waved. Ellen watched a woman drag a little boy away. She heard him wailing, "But I wanna see the clowns!"

Just behind Ellen a row of marchers were holding up a long banner with the word "Freedom" painted in wide brushstrokes across it. Whenever there was a lull in the singing they began to chant "Free-dom! Free-dom! Free-dom!" The sound swelled around her. She could feel it like a drumbeat, and then, almost without knowing how it happened, she could hear her own voice pounding out the two syllables: "Free-dom! Free-dom!"

A few rows ahead, four mounted policemen waded into the marchers, halting them at a cross street so that a line of waiting cars could drive through. A voice from behind the barricades shouted, "Kill the reds!" Other voices took it up until it became a chant. "Kill the reds! Kill the reds!" Ellen wanted to cover her ears with her hands, but they were holding up her sign.

She saw something sailing through the air. A rock? She began shaking. She heard a groan, then screams. One man leapt over a wooden barricade and started punching one of the marchers. Then other people from the sidelines started jumping over the barricades, hitting out at heads, chests, stomachs, backs.

There were no more cars waiting to cross, but the

policemen on horseback held the marchers at a stand-still. "We're trapped!" Mr. Gerson said. "Here, take Mikey." Swinging the child down from his shoulders, he thrust Mikey at Mrs. Gerson and pushed his way into the confusion up ahead.

"Jess, no!" Mrs. Gerson shouted.

"Daddy!" Ellen cried. Why don't they *do* something? she thought frantically.

Her aunt Sonia put an arm around her and shouted, "Freedom! Freedom! Freedom!" Some of the marchers around them joined in, but Ellen couldn't get the word out. She caught a glimpse of the face of one policeman. Perched on his horse, he was looking down at the fight below him with a sort of half smile around his lips. Then she understood. The policemen wanted the marchers to get hurt.

"All right. Break it up. Break it up," one of the policemen shouted at last. Other policemen appeared on foot and forced everyone who had been caught in the melee to the side. The mounted policemen moved back and waved the marchers ahead. Some of the marchers were sitting at the curb beside their broken signs. A policeman stood over them.

When Mr. Gerson worked his way back to his family, his shirt was torn and there was a dribble of blood on his forehead. "Oh, Jess, you're hurt!" Mrs. Gerson cried.

"No, no, it's nothing," he said. "But just wait and see. Our people will be arrested for inciting to riot, and those creeps will get a pat on the head."

Some of the marchers had taken up the freedom

11

chant again, but Ellen's head was still echoing the other chant: "Kill the reds, kill the reds!" The Rosenbergs are reds, she thought. And so are my parents.

Ellen couldn't remember when she had first heard her parents call themselves reds—she might have been five or six. She had wondered what it meant. Were they Indians? She had stared at her reflection in the bathroom mirror—fair skin with a sprinkling of freckles across the nose, root-beer-colored eyes, light brown hair that curled around her cheeks. She was definitely a paleface. But red people were Indians. Finally she had asked her mother, "What tribe do we belong to?"

It had taken Mrs. Gerson awhile before she had understood Ellen's question, and when she did, she had laughed. Being red, her mother had told her, meant that the Gersons and people who believed as they did wanted to make the world a better place for everyone to live in, not a world divided into rich and poor, white and black, but one in which each person would have what he needed to live in peace and harmony.

It had sounded good to Ellen. "Isn't that what everyone wants?" she had asked.

"No," her mother had said. "I'm afraid not."

"But why?" Ellen had persisted.

"It's complicated, Ellen," Mrs. Gerson had said. "Let's just say most people in America are not ready to listen."

It had been confusing to Ellen as a young girl. Her parents were good. She was sure of that. But being red was bad. Red was another word for communist, she learned. And communists got arrested.

Growing up, Ellen felt she had to be very careful to keep her parents' secret. Sometimes she made mistakes and almost gave them away. One of those times had been in third grade when her reading group was gathered around a table in the back of the room.

Someone stumbled on a word in the story and her teacher, Mrs. Ashley, pronounced it: "*Petition*. Does anyone know what *petition* means?" she had asked.

Ellen had raised her hand. "Petition," she began, "like a peace petition . . ." As she said the words she had a terrible thought. Peace petitions were somehow linked with being red. Just the week before, she and her mother and her mother's friend Gertie had stood on one of their town's street corners with an antiwar petition and a man standing nearby had said, "Why don't you commie reds go back to Russia where you belong!"

Ellen had clamped her mouth shut, leaving her words dangling in midsentence. Had anyone heard?

Bobby Nemeth, who sat opposite Ellen, had jumped from his seat, waving his arm for attention. "I know, I know," he yelled. "A petition is sort of a wall that goes halfway up. My aunt has one in her living room."

Mrs. Ashley hadn't looked at Ellen—perhaps she hadn't heard her. "Good try, Bobby," she had said. "But you're thinking of *par*tition. Now, a *pe*tition is . . ."

Ellen had been uneasy for days afterward. Would

she come home from school one day to find her parents missing and a newspaper headline tacked to her front door: "Daughter Betrays Commie Parents"? That was the awful thing about having parents who were red. You just never knew what might happen. Ellen hadn't known then, when she was eight, and she still didn't know now that she was twelve.

Ellen's arms were aching from holding up her sign. She shifted it to her other hand and leaned it on her shoulder. She was just about to cross a street when two mounted policemen turned their horses into the line of march and brought it to a stop, the way they had done earlier. One was so close to Ellen that she could have reached out and touched the polished black boot that rested in the horse's stirrup.

She craned her head back to see the policeman's face. His eyebrows formed a dark ridge just below the brim of his cap, shadowing his eyes. Ellen shivered. What if someone threw a rock at her now? Would the policeman smile and look away? But there were no people yelling at this stop, and when his eyes met hers, he winked. Then, once the cross traffic had driven through, he nudged his horse's side with the toe of his boot and moved aside, motioning the marchers on.

It wasn't until several blocks later that Ellen saw more people gathered behind the barricades. A man up ahead was holding a sign and waving it at the marchers. Ellen was too far away to be able to read it, but automatically she slowed her pace. Her aunt linked her arm through Ellen's and said in her ear, "Don't look at him,

El. Just keep walking. Sing with me," she urged. "You have a beautiful voice." And she began: "Oh, freedom, oh, freedom, oh, freedom over me . . ." in her own rich voice.

Ellen joined in, but when she was close enough to read his sign, her words faltered. "Burn the Spies!" it said. He waved it in her direction and yelled, "Filth! Scum! Commie bastards!"

Ellen couldn't wrench her eyes from his. And he seemed to Ellen to be staring at her, too, his blue-gray eyes boring into her own. She was almost even with him now, and she watched his mouth opening and closing as he spat out his words, a bead of saliva on his lower lip. Drawn on by her aunt, she walked past him.

"Wasn't he ugly!" Ellen said, when he was safely out of sight. The thought gave her a certain feeling of satisfaction.

"I don't know about that, El," Aunt Sonia said. "What frightens me is how *commonplace* he was. Probably a good father who plays with his kids and takes them to the circus every year. It was all that hate that made him into a monster."

Ellen didn't want to think about her aunt being frightened. Aunt Sonia was supposed to be fearless.

She was tired now and wished the march would end. Something sharp was pressing against her little toe. She stopped and sat down on the curb. The street was littered with discarded leaflets and other papers. Her eyes strayed over their words without registering their meaning. "McCarthyism: A Study in Paranoia."

"The Hoax of the Red Menace." Ellen yawned. She pulled off her shoe and shook it. A pebble plinked out and rolled into the gutter. She began to stand up again when a torn piece of paper caught her eye and she picked it up.

There were no words on the paper, only part of a picture of the Rosenbergs' two young sons. She stared hard at the solemn, big-eyed faces for a moment. Your parents are red, she thought. And so are mine. She folded the scrap carefully and tucked it into her pocket. Then she pulled herself to her feet and hurried to catch up with her family.

two

Two days after the march, Ellen sat on the living room floor surrounded by yet-to-be-unpacked cardboard boxes and yet-to-be-untied bundles of books. She was officially on spring vacation—her new school didn't start till the following week—but she had nothing more to look forward to than endless unpacking.

She pulled apart the flaps of one box. Inside was a haphazard jumble—a can opener, oversized spoons, spatulas, a screwdriver, a set of measuring spoons, a half-empty box of birthday candles, some tangled spools of thread. She closed the flaps quickly. It was definitely a "save for Mom" box.

She opened another. Towels, washcloths, sheets—not very interesting. She added it to the growing "save for Mom" collection. This is hard work, she thought. She opened one more. Records. That was more like it. The record player was already unpacked. She picked out a record, slipped it from its case and put it on the Victrola. Then she looked up. Where was Mikey? "What are you doing, Mikey?" she called.

In answer she heard a giggle, then a click as the

latch on the screen door opened. Oh, no. Not again! she thought. "Mikey! Get back here!" she yelled, and jumped up and ran after him.

Mikey was fast, but his stubby legs were no match for Ellen's long ones. Just as he reached the end of the driveway, she caught him by the wrist, lifted him bodily, and faced him back toward the house.

"Yuns gawn up street?"

The voice came from behind her. Ellen turned and stared into the eyes of a girl exactly her height. "Excuse me?" Ellen said, hefting Mikey's compact solidness to her hip. "What did you say?"

"Yuns gawn up street," the girl said again, pointing toward the end of the curved road.

"Oh. No." Ellen shook her head. "We're not going anywhere. I was just trying to catch this monster." Ellen nodded toward Mikey, bent backward now from his waist and ramming his head into Ellen's thigh.

The girl's eyes flicked to Mikey who, upside-down, offered her his most charming grin. The girl smiled, then turned back to Ellen. "Yuns moved in on Saturday, right?"

"Yes," Ellen said. The new girl's speech wasn't really so hard to understand, she decided. "My name is Ellen," she said. "And this is Mikey." Mikey wriggled against her arm, but Ellen knew better than to loosen her hold on him.

"Hi-iii," the girl said, drawing the word out to two syllables. "I'm Judy Dean. I come by on Monday, but I didn't see no one," she continued.

"Oh, yes. I mean no," Ellen stumbled. "We went to a mar . . ." She stopped. "We went to the city," she said.

"The city," Judy echoed, her eyes widening. "I only been to Philly once and all's I remember is a big bell with a crack in it. Did you see it?"

"No, we didn't," Ellen said. Now she had to make another decision: Should she tell Judy that the city they went to was New York, not Philadelphia? Ellen decided not to correct her. She was afraid that New York, like peace petitions, was somehow linked with redness. Ellen kicked a pebble loose from the packed dirt beneath her feet. It seemed that almost every word held a hidden, possibly dangerous meaning. What could she say that was safe?

The brief silence was broken by the creaking screen of the house directly across the street. A big woman with a head full of pink curlers called "Ju-dee, June Bug, Ju-dee! Luh-unch!"

"That's my mom. Gotta go," Judy said. She waved toward Ellen with a hand that ended in sharply tapered red nails. "Why'ncha come by later?" she said. Then she glided away as though she were a model slinking down a runway instead of a kid crossing the straggly patches of new grass on her front lawn.

Ellen watched Judy disappear into her house. Then, with Mikey still on her hip, she trudged across her own lawn, pulled open the screen door, and locked it behind her. "Now you can't get away," she said, and lowered Mikey to the floor. He waddled over to the kitchen cabinet and began pulling out the pots and pans that Ellen had just unpacked that morning. Then he crashed the lids together, hooting in delight.

"Oh, Mikey. You're impossible," Ellen said. She looked at the clock; it was 11:45. Her mother was at her friend Nora's house. She had said they were going to work on a letter to President Eisenhower, asking him to free the Rosenbergs, but that she'd come back for lunch to check on the children.

Ellen stepped over Mikey and pulled open the kitchen cupboard. She reached for a can of tuna fish, opened it, and emptied it into a bowl. Then she added her secret ingredients: lemon juice, diced celery, mayonnaise, and a spoonful of sour cream. She stuck a finger into the bowl and tasted: a smidgeon tart, maybe, but otherwise perfect.

Ellen loved tuna fish. She made it nearly every day. Whether they lived in Smithburg, Jamesville, Franklin, or Fairmore Hills, it was always tuna fish for lunch.

As she arranged the sandwiches on a plate she thought back to Judy's parting words: "Why'ncha come by later?" Had Judy meant what she said, or were the words just empty toss-aways? If Judy really did want Ellen to "come by," what time should she go? Two? Three?

The real question that made all these details seem so vital pushed itself to the surface: Could Judy be a friend? Ellen tried to recall every word and gesture that she and Judy had exchanged. But the sound of pot lids crashing together made thinking impossible.

"Michael Leon Gerson!" Ellen called. Mikey looked up, then brought the lid down gently. It made a quiet *tiinnng*, then faded to silence. But now another sound intruded—a rhythmic *sssh, sssh*. The Victrola! The record Ellen had played earlier had long since finished and the needle was hissing at the end.

She jumped up and ran to the living room. Lifting the needle, she placed it down gently at the beginning of the record. A deep voice filled the room.

> *Joshua fit the battle of Jericho*
> *Jericho, Jericho*
> *Joshua fit the battle of Jericho*
> *And the wall come atumbling down.*

Ellen sat down on the couch, hugging her knees, and let the music roll over her. After Joshua came "Deep River," then "Danny Boy," "Joe Hill," and finally her favorite, "Ma Curly Headed Baby."

> *Oh, my baby, my curly headed baby . . .*
> *Do you want the stars to play with?*
> *Or the moon to run away with?*
> *They'll come if you don't cry . . .*

She reached for the album cover and stared into the smiling face of Paul Robeson as his voice wrapped her in a cocoon of warmth.

Oh, no, she realized with a start. What if Judy heard this? She was sure that people who liked Paul Robeson were red. She turned the volume down. When the song ended, she slid the record back into its case and tucked it out of sight behind a stack of other records.

The melody of the lullaby, though, kept repeating in her head, so that it took her a few moments to notice that the house was totally silent. Mikey couldn't have escaped again, Ellen thought, and hurried to the kitchen. There he was, asleep, cradling the big soup pot in his arms, his cheek pressed against its rounded bottom.

Ellen disentangled him from his aluminum pillow and scooped him up in her arms. "Did you think he was singing about you?" she said. Mikey was no curly-headed baby. His hair, dark blond and matted with this morning's jam, was straight as could be. She kissed his uptilted nose and carried him to his crib.

Ellen was just walking back toward the kitchen when her mother came in. She eyed the sandwiches on the table. "Mmmm, tuna fish," she said, "just what I was hoping for." She headed toward the living room, stepping carefully through the maze of boxes.

Ellen followed her. "See," she told her mother, waving an arm vaguely around the room, "I did a lot of"—she hesitated, then hit on the perfect word— "*organizing* in here."

"Thanks," Mrs. Gerson said, "I appreciate it," though she didn't sound especially appreciative. "Where's Mikey?"

Ellen backtracked toward the kitchen, sat at the table, and picked up a sandwich. "He fell asleep," she said.

"Asleep? I didn't think he knew what that word

meant," Mrs. Gerson said, sitting down opposite her daughter. She, too, picked up a sandwich half and began to eat.

Ellen laughed, but then she felt a twinge of resentment. "How would you know? I'm the one who's been chasing after him all day," she blurted out.

Mrs. Gerson stopped in midbite and looked up in surprise. "You know how hard it is to get any work done with Mikey around, but if it's too much to ask of you, I'll take him with me next time."

Ellen shrugged. In truth, until today, she hadn't minded taking care of Mikey when her mother was away. But now that she had met Judy, the chore seemed to weigh more heavily, to become an imposition. Ellen wanted to tell her mother about Judy, but Mrs. Gerson had already finished her sandwich and was standing up.

"Sorry I can't stay longer, El, but we have to get that letter in the mail by this afternoon. See you five-ish," she said, and, after a quick peek at the still-napping Mikey and a hug for Ellen, she was gone.

Ellen picked up the plate with the remains of her sandwich on it and carried it into the living room. She switched on the television. Gray zigzags ran madly across the screen. Ellen adjusted the rabbit-eared antenna on top of the set and the wavering lines resolved into a woman rubbing her cheek with a piece of cloth. "I only want the softest diapers next to my baby's tender skin," she crooned. She should try keeping them on Mikey, Ellen thought, as familiar organ chords vibrated through the room and the words "Search for Tomorrow" flashed across the screen.

The opening scene showed Ellen's favorite character, Irene Tate, staggering through a forest. "Jamie," Irene was calling. "Where are you? Jamie!" Her image faded into gray and the scene shifted as the organ struck up again. Nine-year-old Jamie, a smudge of dirt on one cheek, was pushing her way through a tangle of branches and calling, "Mother! Mother!"

Even before the Gersons had moved to Fairmore Hills, Jamie and her mother had been looking for each other, calling back and forth every weekday for fifteen minutes, between the Ivory Snow and Babbo commercials, and they still hadn't been reunited. Ellen was glad now that her mother had left. Though Mrs. Gerson had never told Ellen she *couldn't* watch soap operas, she always made her disapproval clear with her grunts and mutterings about the waste of time. Well, too bad if she doesn't like it, Ellen thought.

She folded herself onto the couch and picked up the last of her sandwich when Mikey wandered in. "Change me," he said, his soaked diaper drooping almost to the floor.

Ellen made a face at him. "Anyone who talks that well shouldn't be wearing diapers."

"Diapers," Mikey repeated, pulling at the wet cloth.

"All right, all right," Ellen said, noting with relief that the singing bubbles of the Ajax commercial had just started. She rushed Mikey into a fresh diaper and

24

shirt. "Now you keep these on, understand?" Ellen said gruffly and shook a warning finger at him. Mikey grinned and shook his finger back at her. Ellen gave in and smiled. She lifted him out of his crib just as the closing chords of music marked the end of the program.

"Thanks, kid," she said to him. "Now I don't even know if Jamie found her mother." She carried him to the kitchen and deposited him into his high chair with a bowl of leftover tuna fish.

Ellen looked up as someone tapped at the kitchen window. It was Judy.

"Coming over?" she asked.

Ellen felt a surge of happiness. "I'll be right out," she called.

When Ellen and Mikey followed Judy into her kitchen Judy's mother was at the sink, scrubbing a pot. Steam rose from the soapy water, beading her face with drops of sweat. "Mom, this here's Ellen," Judy said, "what moved in across the street." She turned to Ellen. "Let's go to my room."

But Mrs. Dean was wiping her hands on the dish towel tucked into her belt and coming forward. She took Ellen's hand in hers. "Well, hi," she said. "What brings you folks here?"

"Ummm . . ." The question caught Ellen off guard. With her hand still trapped in Mrs. Dean's slightly damp one, she shifted her weight from her right foot to her left. She certainly couldn't tell the truth — that they'd moved here because her father had been fired from his last job when his boss found out he was a communist. "My father is going to work at the new steel mill," she said at last. That should be safe.

"Well, join the club," Mrs. Dean said. "Everyone in town works there."

Ellen smiled at her. *Join the club.* Her father had used those same words just a few days ago when they had come to Fairmore Hills. She recalled her first view of the town as they drove over a rise. There, spread below her, was a world of gray rooftops arranged in repeating loops, semicircles, and S-curves and, silhouetted against the sky, a cluster of smokestacks trailing gray smoke. They had driven along the winding roads, past one nearly identical house after another, looking for 12 Daffodil Drive. Her mother had stared around her with a stricken look and breathed, "Oh, my God," while her father declaimed in the ultra-deep tones of a radio announcer, "Welcome, folks, to Fairmore Hills. Here you'll find ten thousand perfectly matched homes designed especially for you, the workers of Fairmore Steel."

"Where do the bosses live?" Mrs. Gerson cut in.

"Please! No questions from the audience," Mr. Gerson said, and continued his smooth patter. "No down payment, low monthly fees. So, join the club. It's the American Dream come true."

Join the club. The words echoed in her mind. But she knew her parents would never be members of this club.

"Did your dad work in a steel mill before?" Ellen

heard Mrs. Dean asking her now. She had finally released Ellen's hand.

"Ummm, no," Ellen answered, wishing Judy's
mother would stop asking questions. As far as she knew
her father hadn't worked in a steel mill before. Maybe
he had, though. Mr. Gerson changed jobs often. Before they moved to Fairmore Hills he had worked in a
machine shop. And before that he had worked in a fac-
tory that produced airplane parts. But Ellen never knew
exactly what her father *did*. When she had asked him,
he told her, "Let's just say I'm an organizer." Was
being an organizer a real job, one she could tell Mrs.
Dean about? Or was it something reds did, something
she had to hide?

Judging by her father, being an organizer meant
going to meetings, forming committees, and talking,
talking, talking. When he didn't stay late after work for
a grievance committee meeting, or go out in the
evening for a union meeting, he brought home groups
of fellow workers who would sit around the kitchen
table, engulfed in a haze of cigarette smoke, and talk.
Ellen listened sometimes as they talked about wages,
strikes, safety conditions, bosses, workers. Her father
looked very handsome to her then, his brown eyes
flashing, his cheeks flushed with the flow of words. He
seemed bigger, somehow, and brighter, as if lit from inside. Ellen could see then that there was something
thrilling for her father about being an organizer. But
she wished he could be something ordinary, like a
salesman or a truck driver. At least "steelworker"

27

sounded like a regular occupation.

So far she didn't think she had made any big mistakes. If only Mrs. Dean would stop asking questions! Mikey saved her. He was playing peek-a-boo with Mrs. Dean from behind Ellen's back, his giggles increasing to shrieks of laughter each time he made himself appear. Mrs. Dean leaned over and scooped him up in her arms. "Hi, bare bum," she said. "I sure don't have to ask whether you're a boy or a girl!"

"Oh, Mikey!" Ellen reddened with embarrassment. "He was dressed when we started out. I just can't—he always—"

"Never mind. I like a boy with a little spirit. He minds me of my Chucky when Chucky was young. You just couldn't keep that boy in clothes. But soon's he turned sixteen, I swear, that's all he thought about. Clothes, cars, and girls—"

"Come on, Mama," Judy interrupted, "I ast her over to visit me, not you."

"You're right. You two go on," Mrs. Dean said. "It's been awhile since I got to baby-sit a little one. I'll mind Spunky here." She brought down a fat jar from the top shelf of the cupboard and took out a gingerbread-man-shaped cookie cutter. Mikey grabbed for it. Judy nudged Ellen. She handed her a bag of potato chips and took two Cokes out of the refrigerator. "Let's go," she said.

"Be good, Mikey," Ellen said. Mikey didn't look up. He was looking instead at the cookie jar, where his arm had disappeared up to the shoulder. When he pulled it out with a victorious shout, his stubby fingers clutched a cookie cutter shaped like a star.

The rooms in Judy's house, Ellen saw, were arranged just like those in her own house. Of the three bedrooms, she and Judy both had the medium-sized one. Judy's room, though, looked nothing like Ellen's. Her walls were a deep rose pink, in contrast to Ellen's, which were off-white. Judy's bedspread, curtains, and the gathered skirt of her vanity table were a shimmery, lilac-colored fabric, splashed with dark purple flowers of cut velvet. The room looked like a picture in a magazine — except for the mess.

The bed and floor were littered with shirts, shorts, movie magazines, bras, Juicy Fruit wrappers, and lace-trimmed panties. The chair, pushed up to the vanity table, held a hump of tossed clothes. Judy took a swig of Coke and, ignoring the jumble beneath her, sank onto her bed. "Here," she said, patting a spot beside her. "You can set on these things."

Ellen perched on the edge of the bed. It wasn't the messiness that bothered her. The Gerson household was usually strewn with magazines, newspapers, and books, and now, of course, there were all those boxes that hadn't even been emptied. But she did feel awkward sitting on Judy's underwear.

"Back home, after they shut down the mine, we lived with my uncle Pete," Judy said. As she talked, she idly twisted a thick chestnut curl of hair around her finger. "Me and my cousins Aileen and Mary Beth slept together." Judy took another sip from the bottle and looked around the room, her eyes glowing. "This room is just mine. My mom said I could fix it any way I like. Isn't it nice?"

Ellen nodded. "Purple is one of my favorite colors," she said, which was true. But she wasn't sure she would like to live in such a, well, purple room.

Judy lay back and examined her hands. "Look," she said. "I had ten perfect nails this morning. First time, too. And now one of 'em's broke. Doesn't something like that just make you madder than anything?"

Ellen just smiled in return. She had never thought about having one perfect nail, much less ten, but she was drawn to Judy, her openness, her ease. In a flash Ellen understood a basic difference between them: where Judy assumed that everyone was like her, Ellen assumed that everyone was different.

Judy went on, "Is that too much to ask God for? It wouldn't be hard for Him."

Ellen never knew what to say when people spoke about God. Communists—reds—didn't believe in God. To protect her parents, Ellen had always pretended to believe, but it wasn't easy. She had trouble imagining what it was that people *did* believe. Most people, she decided long ago, thought of God as a man with a white beard, sort of like Santa Claus, but not so jolly. He could pull invisible strings to make rain and snow, sunshine and darkness, happiness and suffering. But even if there were such a God, Ellen doubted he would care very much about Judy's nails. "He probably was too busy with earthquakes, hurricanes, and plane crashes," Ellen said, half-joking.

"That was probably it." Judy nodded seriously. She looked up. "But think about it. All that stuff hurts folks and makes 'em unhappy. Wouldn't it be better, since He has all this power, to use it to make someone happy?"

Ellen, too, had often wondered why a God who was said to love people seemed to spend most of his energies bringing death and disaster to innocent people. "I think you're right," she agreed.

Judy finished her soda and set the bottle down on the floor. "Want some more pop?" she asked. "I'm gonna get me another."

"Pop?" Ellen said, trying to identify the strange word from the context of Judy's clues. "Oh, soda," she translated for herself. She hefted her bottle—full except for her one sip. "No, thanks. I really don't like Coke very much."

Judy looked at her in shock. "You don't like Coke?" she repeated.

As Ellen shook her head, she had a sudden flash of fear. It had to be ridiculous, she thought, but was it possible that people who didn't like Coke were red, that Judy had accidentally discovered the truth?

After a moment Judy asked, "Lemonade, then?"

Ellen said, "Sure." She had admitted that she didn't like Coke, and it was all right. Maybe I can join the club, even if my parents don't, she thought, and smiled.

Judy smiled back. At that moment Ellen saw something that made her shiver. Judy's eyes. They were so beautiful. They were also the same blue-gray color as the eyes that had locked into hers with such hate at the march. If Judy knew her parents were reds, would she look at Ellen like that? Would it be like Aunt Sonia had said—would she turn from an ordinary person into a monster? Ellen couldn't risk that. She had to keep that part of her life secret from Judy.

Judy lowered her gaze to her hands again. "I've been thinking," she said. "This nail polish is the ugliest color. I don't know whatever possessed me to buy it." She held up a bottle of deep purple polish. "Do you think this one's better?"

"Oh, yes. And look," Ellen pointed out, "the purple will match your room."

"Yay-ahhh," Judy said in her drawling way. "Want me to do yours first?"

Ellen looked at her own hands. "Well, I don't know," she said uncertainly. "I don't want to draw attention to my nails."

"Bite 'em, huh?" Judy noted.

"No," Ellen said. "But they look pretty ragged." She hesitated, then held her hands out for inspection.

Judy cast an appraising eye at Ellen's nails. "You have cuticle trouble," she diagnosed matter-of-factly. "I'll help you with it."

Gee, that's not so bad, Ellen thought. She had what she thought was a disgusting habit—she was forever picking and pulling at the skin around her nails, tearing it loose in strips until her fingers bled. But "cuticle trouble"—that sounded much better. "Do you really think you can help?"

"Sure can," Judy said. "And after they're all better, I'll paint 'em same's mine. We can be twins then." She began rummaging beneath the pile of cotton balls and tubes of lipstick until she pulled out a blue plastic case. She unzipped it and dumped out an assortment of surgical-looking tools that were frighteningly like dentists' instruments. Ellen snatched her hands back. "You're going to use those on me?" she said.

"No, on your little brother." Judy laughed. " 'Course on you. You want nails like mine, right?"

"Right," Ellen said. Nails, eyes, mouth, hair—everything, she thought. In just one afternoon, Judy had become Ellen's model.

Judy spent the next hour pushing, poking, scraping, and cutting the ragged skin around Ellen's nails so that, when Ellen returned home with Mikey, her fingers were red, tender, and throbbing with pain. But Ellen didn't care. She felt terrific.

three

*E*llen went to Judy's house again the next day. In her room, Judy opened her closet and pulled out a red circle skirt with a white felt poodle near the hem. She held it up for Ellen. The curls at the top of the poodle's head and end of its tail were masses of French knots. It was the most beautiful skirt Ellen had ever seen.

"I wish I had one like this," Ellen said, running a finger over the springy embroidery.

"My aunt Lou sent me five dollars for my birthday last month and I spent the whole thing on this skirt— four dollars and ninety-nine cents at Lobel's."

"Four ninety-nine," Ellen repeated. She might as well have said four hundred ninety-nine. "All I have is a little over two dollars. And my birthday passed three months ago." She sighed.

She knew her parents didn't have much money. Just last night her mother had sat at the kitchen table adding columns of figures. "Maybe I should try to get some sort of job, Jess," she had said. "Our bills really piled up while you were out of work."

But her father had shaken his head. "No, Mollie.

Fairmore Steel is going to see us through as soon as my paychecks start coming. Anyway," he went on, "you're too valuable to the movement right now."

"All right. But we've got to be very careful. . . ."

Still, being careful didn't mean spending nothing, did it? And she *did* need some things for school—a notebook, some paper. Why not a new skirt?

But her mother shook her head when Ellen brought up the subject. "I'm sorry, Ellen. I can probably scrape up two dollars for some new school supplies. But I don't have extra money to throw away on something as frivolous as a poodle skirt." Mrs. Gerson pronounced the last two words with a heavy emphasis on the "poo," making it sound as though Ellen were asking for something almost dirty.

Ellen blinked back tears. She wasn't sure what *frivolous* meant, but she knew there was no point in arguing. She planned to take the two dollars for supplies. At least she'd be able to get a new notebook, maybe even a bookcover like Judy had—with a picture of Eddie Fisher, the singer, on it.

When Judy knocked at the door the next morning, Ellen was ready. She had $4.23 in her pocket and she intended to spend every penny. She had looked up *frivolous* in her parents' fat dictionary and discovered that it meant "of little or no importance." Well, I say poodle skirts are *very* important, Ellen thought angrily. If she couldn't buy a poodle skirt, she wanted *something* frivolous—just to get back at her mother.

They pedaled their bikes the three miles to the

Fairmore Hills Shopping Center. With Judy leading the way, they coasted through the parking lot and left the bikes in the metal racks at the edge of the lot. Ellen looked around in awe. She had never seen so many stores at one time before—two long rows of them, with a cement walkway making a wide swath between them.

"This way," Judy said. She pulled open the door of Sarton's Variety and made straight for the cosmetics counter. Together they studied the color charts of nail polish and lipstick shades. Judy paid twenty-nine cents for a tube of Plum Passion lipstick to match her nails. She looked at Ellen. "You gonna get one?" she asked.

Ellen fingered the three dollar bills in her right pocket and the $1.23 in change in her left. She hesitated. She could just imagine her mother's expression if she spent the money on makeup. Talk about frivolous! Still, the Peach Nectar Surprise *was* a pretty color. . . .

"All right," she said, feeling reckless. "I will." She reached into her pocket for a quarter and a nickel and received in exchange one penny and a small bag containing her very first lipstick. She and Judy sprayed each other from the sample atomizer of perfume and then left the store reeking of "Evening in Paris."

They walked past the stationery store, barber shop, and hardware store before stopping in front of the pet shop. Four long-eared puppies were climbing over each other, tumbling and rolling in a squirming mass of coffee-colored fur. "Oooooh." Ellen and Judy breathed out the syllable at the same time. "Aren't they cute."

"I wonder what they cost," Judy said.

Taking up Judy's question, Ellen started to sing.

> *How much is that doggie in the window?*
> *The one with the waggly tail,*
> *How much is that doggie in the window?*
> *I do hope that doggie's for sale.*

"Hey, El, you sound just like Patti Page," Judy said.

Patti Page! Her voice could be heard singing that song almost every time someone turned on a radio. She was so . . . American. "Do I really?" Ellen asked.

But Judy was already pulling her away from the window and across the walk to Lobel's, a three-story building. Once inside, Judy steered Ellen past counters of pocketbooks and scarves toward the escalator at the center of the store.

"Did you ever ride one of these?" Judy asked. "The first time I came here I spent half a day just going up and down."

Ellen had been on an escalator before. A couple of years ago her parents had taken her to a demonstration of some sort in New York City. Ellen had had to pee so badly she thought she might have an accident right on Broadway. Finally she and her mother had dashed into Macy's, where they had ridden an escalator from one floor to another until they reached the fifth, where the ladies' bathroom was. All Ellen could think was not how exciting it was but how slow. "I was on one once," she said. But when she saw disappointment cloud Judy's face, she added, "It was a long time ago, though, and it was a creaky old thing with wooden slats. This one's much nicer."

Judy smiled. "Come on, then. Let's go up," she said.

On the second floor they walked through the displays of rugs, fabrics, and towels. When they came to the furniture section, Judy made for a flounced canopy bed. She lay back on the pillows, one arm behind her head, and cooed, "I'm Rita Hayworth, famous movie star."

Ellen lingered over a living room set—a brown couch and two orange chairs separated by a coffee table of blond wood, which held an orange ashtray and two magazines—a copy of *Look* and a copy of *Life*. Ellen sat in one of the chairs and leaned back, trying to imagine what it might be like to live in an ordinary family, one that went to church on Sundays, subscribed to big picture magazines, and had a perfectly matched living room like this. She closed her eyes.

"Come on, daydreamer. Let's go downstairs," Judy's voice broke in.

They rode the escalator back to the main floor, where they wandered through racks of blouses, dresses, and skirts, Ellen didn't see anything like Judy's red circle skirt. Her disappointment was tempered with relief. If it wasn't for sale she couldn't buy it anyway.

Everything looked summery—lightweight and pale colored. She pulled out a yellow-and-white polka-dot skirt with a matching yellow patent-leather belt and checked the price tag: $7.99. "Are they kidding?" she said, laughing. She put the skirt back on the rack and turned to Judy. "Where are the notebooks and things like that?" she said.

As she followed Judy toward the back of the store, something caught her eye. Jammed among a rack of dark, heavy-looking clothes marked "Clearance—50% Off," she saw a glint of blue. She stopped short. It was the rhinestone eye of a poodle appliquéd to the hem of a circle skirt identical to Judy's, except that this one was navy. "Look!" she called to Judy, waving the skirt high, like a victory flag.

A thick, red-ink slash cut through the $4.99 price tag. Beside it was the new price: $2.50. "Oh! I can't believe it!" Ellen hugged the skirt to herself.

"We'll be twins," Judy exclaimed. Then, ever practical, she said, "Well, try it on. It might not even fit."

But it did fit. Ellen whirled in front of the mirror, making the skirt lift and spin like a platter around her waist. She stopped abruptly so that the fabric fell in gentle folds around her legs. She loved it.

After paying for the skirt Ellen used the rest of her money to buy two book covers, each one picturing Eddie Fisher in a different pose, and a notebook divided into sections with colored plastic tabs extending over the edge. It came with a packet of perforated white paper that could be labeled and then folded to fit inside each of the tabs. Let's see, Ellen planned as she and Judy pedaled home, I'll use yellow for math, blue for English. . . .

She turned into her driveway with Judy right beside her. "Let's show your mom all your stuff," Judy said.

"Yes, let's," Ellen agreed boldly. She pushed open the front door and called out, "Hi, Mom. See, I got everything I wanted!"

She stopped suddenly, with Judy just behind her. Her mother was sitting at the kitchen table, a cup of coffee in her hands. Sitting across from her was a heavyset gray-haired man.

"Hello, girls," Mrs. Gerson said. "Come in. This is, uh, Mr. Green, an old friend of ours."

"I'm enchanted to meet you both," Mr. Green said. He rose from his seat and bowed, smiling, toward them.

Enchanted, Ellen thought. What a wonderful word. But she resisted the urge to smile back at him and only nodded. She watched coldly as Judy held out her hand and said, "Likewise, I'm sure," as though she were acting in a play.

Mikey edged his way into the group. "Funny face," he said, reaching for Mr. Green's hand.

"Okay, Mikey," Mr. Green said. He lifted his hand and turned his cupped fist to the side, revealing a painted face. He moved the thumb up and down, mouthing the words "How are you?"

"Oh, cute!" Judy said. "I'm just fine, thank you."

Ellen kept her mouth in a tight line. Maybe that trick amused Mikey, and even Judy, but it would take more than that to win her favor.

40

She was used to having unknown visitors. Sometimes they would only stay for supper or overnight; other times they'd hang around for a week, even a month. Ellen knew, without having any proof, that these visitors were communists—reds—who were underground, in hiding. It had always been that way in her family, and Ellen had never thought much about it. Until now.

Now that they lived on 12 Daffodil Drive, in a house that looked like everyone else's house; now that her father worked in the steel mill, like almost everyone else's father in Fairmore Hills; and especially, now that she had met Judy, she didn't want people like Mr. Green in her house.

She did her best to ignore his presence. "Well, do you want to see what I bought?" she said to her mother, and proceeded to unwrap her purchases. Judy wandered toward the living room while Ellen was displaying her notebook. Ellen had a sinking feeling as she thought of the perfectly coordinated room she had seen in Lobel's—so different from the Gersons' secondhand couch and chairs, their coffee table made of an old door perched on two orange crates, their bookcases of bricks and boards.

Her feeling of discomfort changed suddenly to one of panic. Mikey must have handed Judy his favorite record to put on. Ellen stifled a groan as she heard the familiar voice of Pete Seeger. She bolted into the room, then stopped, frozen, at the sight of Mikey, bouncing in time to the music. Pete Seeger. Didn't everyone know he was red—or at least pink? Judy, at least, didn't seem to. She was clapping in time to Mikey's dance and laughing at him.

"Oh, no," Ellen said, just under her breath. She had just glanced at the coffee table. It was even worse than she imagined—piled high with copies of the *Daily Worker* tied into bundles. The banner headline was clearly visible—the words "Don't Let Them Die!" were spelled out above a photograph cut off below the eyes by the fold of the newspaper. But Ellen was sure that anyone who glanced at it would know the picture was of Julius and Ethel Rosenberg. She wanted to throw herself across the newspapers to shield them from Judy's eyes. But that would only call attention to them. Instead she sidled over to the table, and as casually as possible, she picked up two of the bundles and hauled them into her parents' bedroom. She hurried back for the third bundle and carried that one out, too. When she came back to the living room, the record was just ending. She went to the record player, lifted the record from the turntable, and slipped it into its case. Quickly, she tucked it away among the other records.

Flushed and out of breath, she looked around her. What now? Judy was standing in front of the bookcase, looking directly at *Red Star Over China*. Ellen closed her eyes. There was nothing she could do. When Judy turned to her, though, all she said was, "I like the way your mom mixed all these different-colored books. It looks real nice."

Amazing, Ellen thought. She's not even reading

the titles! Almost giddy with relief, Ellen let herself relax. She unwrapped the packet of perforated tabs that came with her notebook and began separating them. She carefully printed the letters S-O-C-I-A-L S-T-U-D-I-E-S on one, then slipped it into the opening of the green cellophane tab. Judy sat down next to her as Ellen reached for a second label. E-N-G, she printed, happily intent on making each letter as perfect as possible. Maybe things weren't so terrible after all.

Mikey, who had disappeared into the back room, reappeared now, holding a picture book. "Read me," he said to Judy. He climbed onto the couch and settled himself beside her.

"All right," Judy said. Turning the book right side up, she read the title: *"The Little Red Hen."*

The suddenness with which Ellen lifted her head made her hand skid in a jagged line across her label. She moaned inwardly. Of all his books, why did he have to bring *that* one? She put down her pen and listened as Judy opened the book and started to read.

> One day the Little Red Hen found a grain of wheat.
> "Who will help me plant this wheat?" she said.
> "Not I," said the Goose.
> "Not I," said the Cat.
> "Not I," said the Dog.
> "I will, then," said the Little Red Hen.
> And she did.

Ellen prodded the raw skin at the base of her

thumbnail. "Hey." Judy nudged her with an elbow. "You're gonna undo all my work." Ellen pulled her finger away. But her tension increased as Judy read on.

> "Who will help me cut the wheat?" said the Little Red Hen.
> "Not I," said the Goose . . .

I've got to do something, Ellen thought.

Judy continued reading. The Little Red Hen threshed the wheat, took it to the mill to be ground into flour, and baked it into a loaf of bread, all without any help from Goose, Cat, or Dog. Judy came to the last page.

> "Who will help me eat the bread?" said the Little Red Hen.
> "*I* will," said the Goose.
> "*I* will," said the Cat.
> "*I* will," said the Dog.
> "No. *I* will," said the Little Red Hen.
> And she did.

"Whew." Judy closed the book. "The end," she said.

But, just as Ellen feared, Mikey opened the book again. "More," he said.

"Hey, kiddo, not me. One book a day. That's my limit," Judy said, laughing.

But Mikey stood there, holding the book and waiting. Ellen had to act. She jumped up, scattering her labels on the floor, and caught Mikey up in her arms.

"I'll get rid of him," she said. Carrying him toward the bedroom, she whispered in his ear, " 'For those who labor shall be fed.' And that's why they call her Red."

It was a line Mr. Gerson had added as a joke. She knew that, for Mikey, the story wasn't finished until he heard it. But she couldn't let Judy hear it. After all, if the Gersons read their children stories about communist chickens, they must be communists.

She sat Mikey down in front of his bookcase, pulled out *The Tall Book of Mother Goose,* and thrust it into his hands. That should be safe. She left him there and returned to the living room. Walking past her mother and Mr. Green, who were still at the kitchen table, she felt anger, like a bitter taste, rise in her throat. She wanted to spit it out at her mother, to shout at her, "Why do you have to make things so hard for me? Why can't we be like other people?" But Judy was waiting in the living room. She swallowed her words and rejoined her. Gathering up her strewn labels, she reached for her pen and began again. E-N-G-L . . .

four

Mr. Green left the next day after breakfast. He wasn't so bad, really, Ellen had decided. In fact, he was nice. Though her mother had suggested Ellen let him use her room, he had insisted on sleeping on the living room couch. And, instead of spending the whole evening talking boring politics with her parents, he took out a deck of cards and did magic tricks. He even showed her how to do one that ended each time with the cards in four piles, a queen on top of each one. "You see," he told her, "the women always come out on top."

She was almost sorry when he left. She stood at the window and watched as he walked down the street carrying his battered satchel. "Where will he go now?" she asked her mother.

"I don't know, El. That's not something we ask," Mrs. Gerson said.

"Well. I hope he'll be all right," she said.

He had just disappeared around the curve when the phone rang. She heard her mother's "Yes . . . I understand. Don't explain . . . of course. You're always welcome . . . fine. See you later," then the click of the receiver being replaced. Her parents' telephone conversations often sounded like shorthand. Phones, she knew, were not to be trusted.

Ellen's liking for Mr. Green had vanished. "Who's coming now?" she said. "Mr. Brown? Mr. Purple? Why can't they hide out in someone else's house?"

Mrs. Gerson stared at Ellen. "I'm surprised at you. It's little enough, I think, to offer a meal or a bed to a comrade."

Ellen lowered her eyes under her mother's gaze, but she didn't apologize.

"Anyway," her mother continued, "the people coming tonight are our old friends Sam and Allie Baker, and their son, Greg. You remember them, don't you?"

Ellen shook her head, though she did, in fact, remember them.

"Well, anyway," her mother continued, "it sounded as if Sam was forced out of his job just the way your father was. I don't think their presence for dinner will ruin your life."

Ellen shrugged. Maybe this time she was in the wrong, but she couldn't say she felt sorry. "Can I go to Judy's now?"

"I suppose so," Mrs. Gerson said.

Ellen left the house and spent the afternoon listening to Eddie Fisher records and flipping through *Modern Screen* magazine. Judy painted Ellen's toenails Scarlett O'Hara Red. "I've never had my toenails

47

painted before," Ellen admitted, wiggling her toes with pleasure.

"Ooooh, virgin toenails," Judy teased, and both girls collapsed in gigglcs.

At five o'clock, her anger spent, Ellen wandered back to her own house. Her mother, preparing her usual company meal of roast chicken, was just putting the pan in the oven. "I'll set the table," Ellen said.

Setting the table was something Ellen always enjoyed. The Gersons' assortment of dishes was as haphazard as their furniture, but Ellen liked making pleasing combinations of patterns and colors, folding the napkins precisely, lining up the silverware.

When she was finished, she looked at her results. She knew just what was missing. There were three daffodils at the side of the house. She went out and picked them, along with several strands of the tapered eel-like leaves that clustered around them. When she put the flowers in a water glass and set it in the middle of the table, she thought the effect was wonderful.

She heard the familiar rattle of the car as it pulled into the driveway. Her father was home. Ellen looked out the open window. Mr. Gerson got out of the car slowly and stood up, straightening his back in a series of jerky movements, like a mechanical doll unbending. There were two lines extending from either side of his nose to the corners of his lips that Ellen had never noticed before.

Her mother went out to him. "Guess who's coming! The Bakers!" Ellen heard her tell him, putting an arm around his waist and walking beside him to the house.

"No kidding," her father said. "That's great!" The creases etched into his face a moment before disappeared. He smiled broadly and his step quickened.

I guess the Bakers *are* special, Ellen thought.

It got to be six o'clock, then six-thirty. Their guests still hadn't arrived. The chicken was ready. Mrs. Gerson took it out of the oven and covered it with a piece of aluminum foil, but the skin was already puckering.

Her parents tried to reassure each other.

"They may have had a flat tire."

"Mmmm."

"Or they may have taken a wrong turn somewhere."

"Mmmm."

The sky was streaked with rose and lavender as the hour hand edged toward seven. Starved, Ellen buttered a piece of bread for herself. "I'm going to see if Judy wants to ride around a little, okay?" she said.

"Okay," her mother agreed. "Keep an eye out for the Bakers."

"Me, too. Me, too." Mikey stood with his arms outstretched, waiting to be lifted.

"All right," Ellen said. "But you have to hold on tight and sit up straight."

Mikey nodded solemnly.

Ellen waited while Judy finished drying the last of

her supper dishes, then they wheeled their bikes in lazy circles on the street. Mikey sat behind Ellen, holding her waist.

Now the sky was streaked with stripes of deep pink. "Look, Mikey," Ellen said. "Isn't that beautiful!"

The sunsets over Fairmore Hills were often this vivid. It had something to do with the gases that puffed into the air from the steel mill's smokestacks. "Pollution sunsets," her mother called them. But Ellen loved them. She swept her arm across the sky as though painting it with a giant brush.

"Make it red," Mikey said.

"Okay. Close your eyes." Ellen pedaled slowly toward the end of the street. Then she turned around and headed into the sunset again. The pink had deepened into a rich crimson.

"Open your eyes now, Mikey-boy," Ellen told him. She watched his face light up with pleasure when he looked at the flaming sky.

"Ellen made the sky red," he said.

Mikey believed Ellen could do anything—the thought was almost contagious. Ellen laughed.

They coasted up and down the street, making a game of turning in ever-tightening circles. Mikey leaned into each turn so that the bike tilted toward the pavement. Each time he did it, he hooted with laughter.

"Stop it, Mikey. If you do that again I'll let the bike fall. You'll get hurt," Ellen warned.

Mikey ignored her. At the next turn he leaned in

again, forcing the bike to wobble precariously. Instinctively Ellen forced her weight in the opposite direction, saving the bike from crashing onto the road. Mikey laughed again, and in spite of herself, so did Ellen. She couldn't let the bike hit the pavement just to teach him a lesson. He'll have to learn his own lessons, Ellen thought.

A battered green car had turned into Daffodil Drive and was creeping along the street, slowing to a near stop at each house. "Hey, El. I bet that's your company," Judy said.

Ellen turned her bike around. Three people. A New York license plate. "It must be them," she agreed, and waved to them, directing them to the Gersons' house. Mr. Baker opened his door and beamed at the two girls. "Thank you," he said. "I don't think I've ever had a more attractive welcoming committee. We'll have to come to Pennsylvania more often, eh, Greg?"

Greg, who was reaching over the front seat, backed out of the car holding a guitar. Ellen remembered him as a skinny boy of about eleven when she and her parents had visited the Bakers at their New York City apartment.

But that had been about six years ago. He didn't look so skinny now. He nodded and smiled at Ellen and Judy in a general, polite way. Then her parents were running across the lawn and there was a confusion of hugs, kisses, and a jumble of words.

"We were so worried."

"It's impossible to find this place."

"At last."

"We're starved. . . ."

The adults traipsed across the lawn, arms draped around shoulders and waists. Greg followed, and Mikey slid from the back of the bike and took off after them, waddling on his stubby legs.

Ellen, lingering with Judy, watched from the road. "Oooh, is he ever cute," Judy said.

"Mikey?" Ellen asked.

"No, you dope," Judy said agreeably, "Greg. Listen. Tomorrow I want to hear *everything*, okay?"

Ellen laughed. "Okay," she agreed and, waving good-bye to Judy, wheeled her bike up the driveway.

Supper was loud and lively as the grown-ups filled each other in on their doings. "You won't believe what happened to us on the way here," Mr. Baker said. "Wasn't it something?" he said to Greg and his wife, who both nodded.

"I thought I would have a heart attack for sure," Mrs. Baker said.

"So tell us," Ellen's father said.

"Don't rush me, Jess. I don't get to tell many upbeat stories anymore. Well . . ." Mr. Baker took a breath. "We were approaching the tollgate on the bridge over the Delaware. All of a sudden a fleet of police cars surrounded us, red lights flashing. I thought we were going to be arrested for transporting dangerous literature across state lines or something. Well, guess what happened." Mr. Baker stopped and looked from one face to another.

"What?" Ellen prompted.

"Some big official came over to the car, stuck his hand out, and said, 'Congratulations! You're the one-millionth car to cross the bridge!'" Mr. Baker threw back his head and laughed. Everyone around the table laughed, too. But when the laughter faded, the atmosphere in the room had somehow changed. Mr. Baker cleared his throat and shook his head.

"You heard about Dan, I suppose," Mrs. Baker said. "The FBI picked him up right at the Mexican border."

Mr. and Mrs. Gerson nodded. "And Ted had to go into hiding," Mrs. Gerson put in.

It was quiet then for a few moments until Mrs. Gerson sighed and said, "Well, you may as well tell us about your news."

"There's not much to tell," Mr. Baker said. "I was fired."

For the first time, Greg spoke. "The entire country is kowtowing to the McCarthyites."

Mrs. Baker nodded. "The college told Sam they had no choice. They, quote, deeply regretted their action, unquote, but unless he signed the loyalty oath, they would be forced to let him go."

Mr. Baker gave a short laugh. "No one asked me to sign a loyalty oath when I was sitting in a foxhole in Italy, making the world safe for democracy. But to teach Hamlet to college sophomores . . ." His voice trailed off.

Mr. Gerson asked, "Did you get any support from

any of the other teachers? You had some good friends on the faculty."

"Support! Friends!" Mrs. Baker almost shouted. "With such friends who needs enemies!"

"Come on, now, hon. It's not so easy to take an unpopular stand. People are scared," Mr. Baker said.

"That's right, Allie," Greg added. "I'm lucky. I have friends at school who come from the same kind of background as I do. There are lots of red diaper babies at City College. But I can imagine that it must be very hard if you're alone. You can either speak out and be ostracized or keep quiet and feel as though you're betraying yourself."

Listen to him, Ellen marveled. *Kowtowing . . . ostracized.* He even calls his mother Allie! She looked at Greg with awe as the words of the others continued to float around her.

" . . . people have families," she heard Mr. Baker say. "They're frightened—"

"Oh, Sam," Mrs. Baker interrupted, a hard edge to her voice. "Why do you have to make excuses for everyone?"

The air was thick with tension. Ellen saw her parents exchange glances. Her father patted Mrs. Baker's hand. "Sam is right, you know. It's as though there were a machine out there manufacturing fear. Teachers can't teach. Actors can't act. Writers can't write. The Weavers singing 'Goodnight, Irene' threaten national security." He laughed. "But Eisenhower is still smiling, so I guess things can't be too bad."

"You must be right," Mrs. Baker muttered. She managed a sad smile.

Mikey was pulling at his ear, the only reliable sign that he was ready for bed. "Let me tuck him in. Then we can relax and have coffee," Mrs. Gerson said. She picked him up and carried him toward his bedroom, with Mikey blowing kisses over her shoulder like a departing movie star.

"I'll do the dishes," Ellen said. Everyone else meandered into the living room. When Ellen finished washing up and joined the others, Greg was on the floor, strumming his guitar softly, his back against the couch. She picked a spot across the room from him and watched his fingers drum staccato patterns along the bridge of the guitar.

Mrs. Gerson had tiptoed from the back room into the kitchen and entered now, carrying a pot of coffee and a tray of cups, saucers, and cookies. "Gee, that sounds good," she said, setting down the tray. "Come on, everyone, help yourselves." She fixed herself a cup, sat down on the couch, and leaned her head back. "I can't believe Mikey actually went off to bed without a struggle," she said. "I think I deserve a medal for that."

"Hold the fanfare," Mr. Gerson said, pointing toward the hallway. Mikey stood there, bouncing to the music.

"Oh, well, come here, Mikey-boy," Mrs. Gerson said, laughing. "You might as well join the party." He was passed from lap to lap but wouldn't settle anywhere until he reached Greg. He sat down there, his ear close to the guitar. Greg took Mikey's fat fingers and brushed them over the strings.

"Again," Mikey said, as Ellen knew he would, and Greg let him strum the strings once more.

Her parents and the Bakers were talking quietly together. "Take this name," she heard her father say, handing Mr. Baker a scrap of paper. "He's a good person . . . runs a machine shop . . . may be able to get you a job."

Mr. Baker folded the paper into his shirt pocket. "Thanks, Jess. It's good to know there's someone I can depend on. . . ."

Mr. Gerson dismissed the words with a wave of his hand. "How about another song," he said to Greg. Greg nodded and began to pluck out a melody Ellen hadn't heard before. Then, in a low, slightly husky voice, he started to sing.

What shines from your cell
To my lonely cell
My loved one

What shines from your cell
To my lonely cell
My loved one

Your eyes like bright stars
Shining through prison bars
Your eyes like bright stars
My loved one.

Ellen was caught up by the romantic vision that the song painted. Her eyes filled with tears. She imagined the man and woman separated by iron bars, but united by love.

Then she realized that the song was about the Rosenbergs. She felt a stab of annoyance. Couldn't she ever get away from them? She looked at Greg, his dark curls bent over his guitar. The Rosenbergs weren't real, she told herself. They were like storybook characters, they had nothing to do with her. Greg was real, though, and Ellen longed for him to lift his head. To look at her.

The coffee her mother had brought in sat forgotten on the table. When the song was finished Ellen passed around cups of coffee to each person. She held out the tray of milk and sugar. When she came to Greg, the pitcher of milk unaccountably clattered against the side of the tray. "No thanks, Ellen," he said, "I take it black."

"Oh. Yes. I do, too," Ellen said. He actually said my name, she thought. She set the tray down and poured herself a cup. In fact, on those rare occasions when she drank coffee, she poured about an inch of it into a tall glass, stirred in a tablespoon or so of sugar, and then filled the glass with milk.

She took a sip of the almost black liquid and shuddered. She took another sip. This one tasted even worse—a dark, bitter taste. Did people really like it this way? Did Greg? She stole a glance at him. His cup was already empty. She lifted hers to her lips.

Mikey had fallen asleep where he was, his head lolling against Greg's arm. Mrs. Gerson stooped to pick him up. "Well, I see he gave up. How about you?" she said to Ellen.

"I'm not two years old!" Ellen said, aware that her protest itself sounded whiny and babyish. Now she certainly wasn't going to admit that she was tired, though she had a terrible urge to yawn. She tried to stifle it, forcing her mouth closed by clamping her teeth together, but she couldn't prevent her eyes from filling with water.

"Do you want me to tuck you in?" Mrs. Gerson offered.

Ellen glared at her mother, shooting her poison-arrow darts from her eyes. "No, thank you," she said. "I can tuck myself in." She rose awkwardly, her legs cramped from sitting, and, gathering what felt like her last shred of dignity around her, said "Good-night."

"Good-night, Ellen," Mr. Baker said.

" 'night, dear."

"Good-night . . ."

The chorus pursued her down the hall toward her bedroom.

Ellen completely covered herself with her sheet and thin blanket, but she could still hear the murmur of voices from the living room — too loud to ignore but not loud enough to understand, though she strained to catch the words. She thought, instead, of Greg, and she repeated his words to herself. "No thanks, Ellen, I take it black. . . . No thanks, Ellen . . ." He said my name . . . My name. Shutting her eyes and curling herself into a tight ball, she remembered the way Greg had looked with his head bent over his guitar. He never had raised his head to look at her and now, though she tried her hardest, she could not recall his features. She tossed under her blanket. Suddenly it was of utmost importance that she see his face. How else could she remember him? I can just say I'm thirsty, she thought. On my way to the kitchen, I'll get a glimpse of him.

Now that she had made her decision she felt better. She pushed the covers back and stood up. Feeling her way to her doorway, she started down the darkened hall. But before she reached the kitchen she was stopped by her mother's voice. Huddled against the wall, she listened.

"Yes, it's gotten very bad. We really feel it's important to do something about the kids."

"The kids"? Ellen dug her nails into her palms and strained to hear the next words over the pounding in her ears. Now her father spoke.

"You've been our closest friends since college a million years ago. Would you be guardians of Ellen and Mikey—in case something happens to us?"

Ellen heard Mrs. Baker say, "You know we'd do anything for you. You don't even have to ask."

And Mr. Baker said, "Of course, of course."

Then the talk turned to another topic and Ellen, her original mission forgotten, stumbled back to her room. The phrases she had just heard swirled in her head. " . . . do something about the kids . . . be guardians . . . in case something happens . . . do something . . . in case . . ." She held her hands over her ears and rocked her head from side to side, trying to blot out the words.

But it was no good. Powerless against them, she switched on her night-light and reached under her bed for her worn copy of *A Tree Grows in Brooklyn.* She riffled through its pages until she found the piece of paper she had tucked in there after the march. She stared at it hard now. The eyes of the Rosenbergs' sons, Michael and Robert, held her fast, confronting her in silent argument.

"We are like you."

"No."

"The same thing that happened to our parents can happen to yours."

"No."

"The same thing that happened to us can happen to you."

"No. No. No!" Ellen screamed silently. She crumpled the paper in her hand and the accusing eyes disappeared within its creases. But she couldn't escape the truth: Her parents would abandon her before they would abandon their cause. She was alone in the world.

five

When Ellen awoke the next morning she had to unwind herself from a tangle of sheet that had somehow wrapped around her during the night. She rubbed her eyes. Something was pressing on her like the memory of a bad dream. Then she remembered. It wasn't a dream. The conversation she had overheard was real.

She got herself out of bed, washed and dressed automatically. She peeked into Mikey's room. He was asleep, humped in his usual rear-in-the-air position. There was no sign of the Bakers. They must have left late last night, Ellen thought.

She wandered into the kitchen. Her parents were there, her father drinking coffee, her mother writing at the table amid a clutter of last night's coffee cups. Ellen watched her as she lifted her pencil from the page, chewed its end for a moment, then bent over the paper again and wrote some more.

Mrs. Gerson raised her head. "Hi, Hon," she said. Her father echoed, "Hi."

"Hi," Ellen said. She began to transfer the cups

from the table to the sink, carrying one cup per trip. Each time she deposited a cup in the sink she clinked it against the others as noisily as possible without breaking it. But Ellen's efforts to draw her parents' attention failed. Her father excused himself from the table and left the room. When her mother did look up she gave Ellen a casual smile before bending over her writing again.

Her mother's apparent contentment made Ellen feel even worse. Now that her parents had "done something about the kids," had disposed of them with barely the blink of an eye, they were free to write leaflets, organize unions, march in protests, go to jail, put their lives on the line. And Ellen knew that she, a mere daughter, couldn't compete with the Idea, with communism.

There were many times when Ellen wished that her parents were more commonplace, more like the parents she saw on television or read about in books. But until yesterday, whatever they were, she had belonged to them. Now she felt cast off, set adrift on a cold sea. What was she going to do?

She filled the sink with hot, sudsy water, picked up a cup, and rinsed it out.

I'm twelve and a quarter years old, she thought. She couldn't leave home. Anyway, where would she go? Her parents did give her a place to stay and food to eat, even if they didn't really *see* her. She picked up another cup and sloshed it around in the soapy water. And Mikey, she thought, I couldn't leave him. Well, then, what do I want? The answer came: I want to be an ordinary American girl. Like Judy.

Having set this goal, she felt a little better. In a spurt of energy she quickly finished the dishes and ran to her room. She sat down on her bed with a pencil and her new notebook.

Using Judy as her model, she would make a list of the characteristics of an ordinary girl, she decided. She had known Judy for only a few days, but she could at least make a start. Under the heading "Judy Likes" she wrote,

1. Chewing gum
2. Wearing makeup
3. Anything purple
4. Dirty jokes
5. Circle skirts

She looked at Number 1: Chewing gum. Judy had a real gift for that, especially for blowing bubbles. She could blow tiny bubbles, the size of peas, and medium-size bubbles, shiny as Christmas bulbs. Most impressive, though, were her giant bubbles, so thin they were translucent. They broke softly against her face and molded to her features like a melted pink mask.

When she wasn't blowing bubbles, Judy had a piece of gum in her mouth just for chewing. One stick would last hours as she folded and refolded it against her back teeth, making a sharp cracking sound each time she squeezed out a trapped air bubble. Judy didn't even remove her gum for meals, but tucked it into a hidden recess in one cheek while she ate.

Ellen decided to begin with plain chewing—it looked easier. For plain chewing Judy always used Juicy Fruit. Judy had left a package behind the last time she was at Ellen's. I don't think she'll mind if I use just one piece, Ellen thought. She unwrapped a stick and started to chew. Liquid sweetness oozed out and a wave of nausea rose in her throat. She swallowed. The Juicy Fruit taste was unbearably sweet. She chewed and swallowed, chewed and swallowed. This might be a little harder than I thought, she realized. She took the gum out of her mouth and looked at the other items on her list.

She already had a head start on items 2 and 5, with her tube of Peach Nectar Surprise lipstick and her new skirt. And she had told Judy how much she liked purple. It was number 4 that stumped her. Ellen didn't know where Judy learned all her jokes, but almost every time they got together, she had a new one. Where was Ellen going to learn one? Her parents didn't sit around telling jokes; she had no cousins her age; and her brother was a useless two years old, not a helpful seventeen like Chuck. Chuck hadn't moved to Fairmore Hills with the other Deans but had stayed "back home" to work in a gas station. He called Judy every other day, though, just to give her a new joke.

Ellen was used to finding information in books, and the library might have been a good place to look. The trouble was, it was a weedy lot with a sign announcing "Future Site of Fairmore Hills Public Library."

Ellen didn't have much hope, but she thought she might as well look through the books on her parents' shelves. She scanned the big bookcase in the living room. Nothing. The smaller bookcase. Nothing. The long, low bookcase in the hall. This time she noticed a thin book entitled *The Lure of the Limerick*. She pulled it out and looked at its cover—a line drawing of a mostly naked woman. Thrilled with her discovery, she flipped through its pages. The poems inside weren't exactly jokes, but they certainly seemed dirty. She picked one out and studied it until she knew it by heart.

Her real test, she knew, would come tomorrow, when school started again after the spring vacation. The thought of school filled her with a mixture of dread and excitement. Dread because first days in new schools were always horrible for Ellen, especially when, as now, they came in the middle of the year, when friendships already seemed sealed with glue. Excitement because there was Judy, and the challenge to be like her.

Could she pass? Would she be able to chew her gum in a natural way? Would her lipstick match her skirt? Would her joke be funny—and dirty—enough? Or would her props collapse around her, exposing her as—what was that phrase Greg had used—a red diaper baby, a child of communists, for all to see?

Judy was going to come by at 7:45 on Monday morning. To make sure she had enough time, Ellen had set her alarm for 6:30. She needn't have worried about oversleeping. She was awake most of the night.

She heard the muffled sounds of the late-night news her parents always listened to. She heard her father stumbling around from bedroom to bathroom to kitchen before he left for his 3 A.M. to 11 A.M. shift at the steel mill. She heard the wheezing rattle of the Dugan man's truck, delivering packaged bread and doughnuts. She must have dozed then, because she started awake, bathed in sweat, her heart racing, from an instantly forgotten nightmare. She lay in bed and stared at her gradually lightening room, watching familiar forms emerge—the posts at the end of her bed, the edge of her chest of drawers. There was no point in trying to get back to sleep. She pushed in the button on the back of her clock and got out of bed. She had laid out her clothes the night before; she put them on now—her new circle skirt and a white blouse with a round collar. She went into the bathroom, brushed her teeth, washed her face, and combed her hair.

"Ellen-Ellen-Ellen-Ellen-Ellen!" Mikey's singsong greeting outside the door made her smile.

"Mikey-Mikey-Mikey-Mikey-Mikey," she chanted back at him.

He laughed. "Ubba bubba bubba bubba bubba," he returned.

Ellen, her face pressed into a towel, opened the bathroom door. "Booga mooga looga wooga pooga," she said.

Mikey giggled in delight. "Gubba gubba gubba gubba gubba."

"Enough, Mikey," Ellen said. But he kept on.

"Mugga bugga rugga . . ."

Why, Ellen wondered, did people say that little kids have short attention spans? Mikey could play this game for hours. "Want some breakfast?" she asked him. She knew she wouldn't be able to eat anything. She could already feel her first-day-of-new-school knot in the pit of her stomach. But making breakfast for Mikey would give her something to do.

Mikey nodded. "How about pancakes?" she asked him. Those would be good. Then she could measure and mix and pour and stir without having to think for at least fifteen minutes.

Mikey wasn't cooperating, though. "Jo-jos," he said.

"Oh, Mikey, Cheerios again?" She took the box from the shelf and poured the cereal into a bowl. Ellen heard her mother's waking-up sounds coming from the bedroom. She automatically filled the coffee pot and set it on the stove.

A minute later Mrs. Gerson breezed in. "Good morning! You're both up so nice and early. You must be excited about school, Ellen. New classes, new teachers . . ."

Ellen knew there was no point trying to explain how she really felt. And now it didn't matter so much. She felt disconnected from her parents. She managed a smile.

Mrs. Gerson ate her breakfast quickly. "I've got to drive all the way to Newark to drop off some leaflets," she told Ellen. She lifted Mikey from his high chair and wiped soggy Cheerios from his chin. "Come on, Bubbie, let's get you dressed," she said, and carried him into his room.

Ellen busied herself mopping up milky puddles and stray Cheerios around Mikey's high chair. "See you this evening," Mrs. Gerson said when she returned with Mikey in polo shirt and overalls. She bent to give Ellen a hug. "Have a terrific first day of school."

Mikey ran to Ellen and clung to her leg. "Go school," he said.

"Not today, Mikey," Ellen said. She stroked his head, then tried to pry his fingers loose. He held on.

"No, Mikey, you're coming with me. In the car," Mrs. Gerson called from the door.

Mikey instantly released his hold on Ellen's leg. "Ca, ca," he said.

Ellen got up from the table and waved at them, hurt that Mikey had let go so easily. She looked at the clock. There was still half an hour before it was time for Judy to arrive. She went into the bathroom again and picked up her hairbrush. There was a flip of curl near her temple that refused to lie flat. She wet it and forced it down with a bobby pin. Then she peered into the mirror. Oh, no! A pimple. She stared at the raised red mark just to the side of her nose. The rest of her face disappeared. All she could see was the inflamed blotch.

"How can I go to school like this!" she moaned. She held a washcloth under the hot water tap, then pressed it against the pimple. When she removed the cloth and looked into the mirror again, the swelling was smaller, but the pink area had spread across her cheek. What should I do now? she thought, a feeling of panic rising in her. Maybe I should try cold water. She turned on the cold water tap full force, soaked the washcloth and pressed it to her cheek.

Rap, rap! The metal knocker sounded at the front door. She took the washcloth from her face and raised her eyes to the mirror. If anything, her cheek looked even redder. The knocking sounded again. She dropped the cloth into the sink and went to the door. Judy was standing there, looking perfect in her poodle skirt.

"Are you ready?" Judy said. "If we get to the bus stop early, you can meet some of the other kids."

"I wish I could stay home," Ellen said. "Just look at me!"

"You look good. I like that blouse with your skirt," Judy said.

"But this pimple," Ellen insisted. "Look. It's huge!"

"Where? Let me see." Judy came through the vestibule and into the kitchen. She studied Ellen's face. "Oh, yeah. You been messing with it. I can tell. Don't worry none, though. I'll cover it up so it won't hardly show at all." She reached into her shoulder bag and pulled out her bulging flower-patterned cosmetic kit. "Come on over here in the light," Judy directed.

Ellen obediently moved to the window and raised her face. She felt relieved of her problem now that she had put herself in Judy's hands.

Judy brought out a tube of skin-colored cream. She squeezed a blob of it onto a fingertip and dabbed it on Ellen's cheek, smoothing it in with feathery touches. Then she stood back to study the effect. She frowned, opened a round compact, and buffed powder over Ellen's cheeks, nose, and chin. She scanned the result through narrowed eyes and shrugged. "That's the best I can do. You shouldn'ta fooled with it."

Ellen looked at herself in the compact mirror. The red blotchiness on her cheek had disappeared under the coating of cream. She could still see the pimple near the crease of her nose, but at least it didn't take over her whole face. And if she held her head at a certain angle, no one would notice. "Oh, Judy, it's much better," she said. "You saved my life."

By now there wasn't much time to spare. Ellen picked up her notebook and they left the house. They raced to the end of Daffodil and turned the corner into Dahlia. Ellen glanced at Judy bounding along easily beside her and tried to match her gait. As usual Judy was chewing Juicy Fruit. Maybe I should try again, Ellen thought. "Do you have any more gum?" she asked.

"Sure," Judy said. She reached into her bag and pulled out a stick.

They were half a block from the bus stop now. Ellen could see two boys leaning against the corner mailbox. She slowed her pace so that Judy walked in front. One of the boys whistled, and Judy turned back toward Ellen and grinned. Then without seeming to do anything at all she arched her shoulders, making her chest stick out, and tossed her head so that her brown waves rippled against her back.

A girl with a blond ponytail was running across the street. The three of them reached the bus stop at the same time. "Hey, Louise," Judy said. "This here's Ellen. This is Louise Warski, Ellen."

"Hi." Louise's voice came out between gasps of breath. Like Ellen she was holding a notebook with an Eddie Fisher cover to her chest. It seemed like a good omen.

"Hi," Ellen said and smiled back.

What was the secret ingredient that made this first-day-in-a-new-school so much better than any of her other first days? Ellen wondered. Was it the Juicy Fruit, which she managed to keep in her mouth until her first class started? Was it her Peach Nectared lips? Her poodle skirt? Her regulation notebook? Or was it just knowing that Judy was somewhere in the building? Whatever it was, it was working.

She had had a moment of panic when the bus first pulled in to the circular drive in front of the school, an imposing three-story tan brick building. As everyone herded off the bus, pushing, shoving, shouting, Ellen realized that she had no idea what to do. "Where should I go?" she asked Judy.

"Don't worry none. I'll take you to the principal's office. They'll give you your schedule."

And from then on, everything went amazingly

smoothly. By 12:30 she had been to homeroom, English, science and hygiene. She had even gotten through what was always the most dreaded time — lunch — and actually enjoyed it. As soon as she entered the cafeteria, she heard someone calling her name. Louise was sitting at one of the long tables with another girl, motioning to her. She joined them and said hello to the other girl, whose name, she learned, was Sandy. Busy talking, Ellen still managed to eat most of the food on her tray — some sort of pale meat glazed with a jellylike gravy, a perfectly rounded scoop of mashed potatoes, and a rectangle of orange Jell-O studded with peas and carrots.

She had only three classes after lunch. First there was study hall, which was draggy and boring. She found, though, that if she kept her eyes glued to the wall clock long enough, she would hear a sharp click and then the minute hand would jump ahead two full minutes. It was a small discovery, but it made her feel good. She could see time fly.

She had a wonderful surprise in social studies. Judy was in her class. Sitting in the back of the room with her feet hooked into the rungs of the chair in front and talking to the girl at the next desk, she waved and called out, "Yo, Ellen!" when Ellen came into the room.

Ellen waved back and handed her transfer card to the teacher, Mr. Mitchell. Then she waited for him to assign her a seat the way her other teachers had. But Mr. Mitchell, who had been leaning against the window ledge when she entered, told her, "We just sit where the spirit moves us in here." He had a slow, almost lazy way of talking and he looked at her through heavy-lidded eyes. "It appears you already know someone here. Feel free to sit back in the boondocks with Miss Dean."

Ellen liked his noticing that she was Judy's friend, and she wanted to sit near Judy, of course. But she was sorry Judy wasn't sitting nearer to the front of the room. She would have preferred to be closer to Mr. Mitchell. She watched him as he moved about the room conducting his lesson, his hands in his pockets. What was it about him that was appealing? He wasn't really handsome. His cheeks were deeply pitted from past acne, his nose jutted out at a sharp angle, and some thin strands of brown hair hung limply on his forehead. But when his eyes, which were deep set and dark blue, met hers for a moment, Ellen felt a rush of warmth. She doodled his name in graceful loops around the edges of her notebook. Mr. Mitchell, Mr. Mitchell . . .

The atmosphere in math, her last class, was very different. The teacher, Miss Howe, nodded curtly to Ellen when she came to her at the start of class. She handed her a textbook and directed, "All right, Miss Gerson, you can take the second seat in the third row." As soon as the bell sounded she clapped her hands twice and said, "Good afternoon, Class. Please open your books to page one thirty-seven. The following students go to the board: Noonan, Konski, Prado, Stephens. The rest of you work on problems one through four at your desks." Not even a "Welcome back, hope you had a good vacation," like the other teachers, Ellen thought, groaning along with the others as she opened her notebook to the yellow-labeled math section.

Suddenly the room shook with the blare of a wailing siren amplified over the public address system. Ellen jumped. The wail petered out, then rose in volume and diminished again. A boy next to her complained, "Oh, no. Not again."

"Is it a fire drill?" Ellen whispered to him.

"No," he hissed back. "Air raid."

The students at the board put down their pieces of chalk and returned to stand by their desks. Everyone else slammed their books shut and stood up. Then, row by row, they began to file out into the hall. Ellen walked out with her row, and copying the pose of those around her, she squatted down in the hall and folded her arms over her head. Behind her an unseen hand pressed on her neck, forcing her forehead to butt into her knees.

What's happening? Ellen thought. She raised her head a bit and saw the corridor lined with huddled bodies, arms cradling heads. A voice barked out, "Heads down over there!" and she lowered hers onto her knees again.

Several minutes passed. Her left foot fell asleep; pins and needles stabbed her sole. Suddenly there was a crackling over the loudspeaker and then the recorded roar of a jet plane, followed by a high-pitched whistling and a *boom*! A man's voice announced, "We are under attack. Enemy planes are dropping bombs on our homes, churches, and schools. Yes, this is just a drill. But remember, it could happen. Russia can attack us at any time. As your principal, I want each and every one of you to be prepared. Wherever you are, when you hear the alert, duck and cover until the all clear sounds."

Ellen curled herself tighter into a ball. Of course she knew that Russia was America's enemy. But she had grown up associating good things with Russia. Her parents and their friends talked about the Russian Revolution in tones of almost worshipful awe. Even Mikey's middle name, Leon, was chosen in honor of one of its heroes—though Ellen couldn't remember which one. One of her favorite records was an album of Russian folk songs. She loved the cover, too. It pictured a laughing young girl wearing an embroidered pinafore, her thick black braids flying behind her as she whirled.

It was all very confusing. She pressed her head to her knees and waited for the all clear to sound.

═══════════ six ═══════════

*T*here was another air raid drill in school the following week. The siren went off halfway through English class, but this time Ellen knew exactly what to do.
She immediately closed her book, stood beside her
desk, and filed out briskly with her classmates. Once in
the corridor she quickly assumed the duck and cover
position, her forehead pressed tight to her knees, and
waited.

Everything went according to pattern. Again there
was the recording of an approaching airplane, then the
explosion and Mr. Slavin's speech. Around her Ellen
could hear feet moving an inch forward or back to ease
a cramped leg, shoulders pushing against the wall to
find a more comfortable position. She visualized the
long hallway as she had glimpsed it that first day, lined
on both sides with the hunched-over bodies of her
schoolmates. What are we doing here? Ellen wondered. Why do we have all these air raid drills?

Ellen was used to fire drills. Every school she had
attended had them, and it was easy to see the reason behind them. But the reasons for air raid drills did not

seem as clear. She knew what Mr. Slavin said—they would keep the children safe from an atom bomb. But wouldn't an atom bomb fall right through the building? And if it did, would it matter whether they were crouching, standing, or running? And who would drop such a bomb? According to Mr. Slavin, it would be Russia. But why would the Russians do that? As far as she knew, the Americans were the only ones who had ever dropped an atom bomb—though it was dropped on Japanese people, not Russians.

And then there was something else. The government said that the Rosenbergs had given the secret of the atom bomb to the Russians. Was that true? Just the other day, when Ellen had been flipping through the newspaper looking for the comics page, the word *Rosenberg* had caught her eye. She had stopped and looked at the article. It showed a copy of a diagram that the government said Julius Rosenberg had given to the Russians—a couple of circles with some lines through it. It reminded her of the drawings Mikey did. Was this the secret of the atom bomb? Did Julius Rosenberg give it to the Russians?

Ellen wanted to blot out all these unanswered questions. She felt certain that ordinary American kids didn't have such thoughts.

Suddenly she heard the tap-tap, tap-tap of staccato footsteps. They sounded louder and sharper as they approached. The back of her neck ached; she had to lift her head. Mr. Mitchell walked briskly past her and continued down the hall. She couldn't be positive, but she was almost sure that he had winked at her. She knew what he was saying with that wink: "You and I know this is silly, but let's go along with it for now." It was easy now to lower her head, her smile hidden between her knees. And, at last, she heard the welcome blast of the all clear.

Judy teased her about having a crush on Mr. Mitchell; Ellen had to admit that it was true. She knew by his wedding ring that he was married, but that didn't interfere with her daydreams. If anything, it prompted more romantic imaginings. She spent hours visualizing his wife in various guises. Her favorite was of a woman who had once been beautiful but was now hideously disfigured, the result of a car accident in which Mr. Mitchell had been driving. Though his love for his wife had died, he remained loyal through guilt and compassion.

It didn't matter, either, that Ellen wasn't alone in her infatuation with Mr. Mitchell. When the bell marking the end of social studies rang each day, most of the students grabbed their books and headed into the thronged hall. But there were usually three or four girls who lingered at Mr. Mitchell's desk—always for a good reason. "I didn't understand our homework assignment." "Is our notebook check *this* Friday?" Ellen was now a member of this gathering. In order to get to math class before the late bell sounded, she had to race all the way to the other end of the building and up one flight of stairs. But the possibility of a word, a glance, a smile from *him* was worth that price.

Ellen entered her social studies room at the beginning of her third week at Fairmore Hills Junior High and saw Mr. Mitchell taping up a picture of an igloo. Next to it he taped one of a mud hut with a thatched roof, then a picture of a grand white building with four fluted columns in front. He continued taping up one picture after another, finishing just before the bell rang.

Mr. Mitchell strode back and forth in front of the pictures, then stopped and faced the class. "What would you say these pictures have in common?" he asked.

There was silence in the room. The answer seemed obvious to Ellen, but she was reluctant to raise her hand. She never liked to draw attention to herself, and answering questions was always a risky business. She looked down at her notebook of Mr. Mitchell doodles and decided to be brave—for him. She raised her hand and, when he nodded, said, "They're all places people live in."

"Very perspicacious, Ellen," he said.

She smiled and blushed. *Perspicacious* sounded to Ellen like the name of a disease, but her answer seemed to be acceptable.

"What's different about them?" Mr. Mitchell asked.

The answer to this question seemed obvious, too, but Ellen wasn't willing to push her luck. She left the question to someone else. Tom Perlis said, "Obviously an igloo is not the same as a mud hut."

"I couldn't have said it better myself," Mr. Mitchell said. "So," he went on, "the point of all this is the subject of our next unit. We're going to study various types of shelters. Why do some folks live in brick houses and others in tents? What do peoples' houses tell us about their surroundings, their lives? I'd like you to work in groups of two or three. Choose a structure and put together a project about it. Take some time now to decide who you want to work with and what your project will be. Then check in with yours truly."

Ellen and Judy exchanged glances. It went without saying that they'd be partners. Judy went directly to the photograph of the big white house. But Ellen was drawn to the picture that looked like her Fairmore Hills house, one that melted in sameness into its surrounding houses—and allowed Ellen to do the same. That was the house that had to be the subject of her project, even if Judy didn't want to be her partner.

She turned and saw Sue Kitchner standing behind her. Tall and almost gawky in her thinness, Sue was pale, with wide brown eyes and straight brown hair. She was so quiet Ellen didn't think she had heard her speak yet except to answer "Here" in a whispery voice when Mr. Mitchell took attendance. Next to her, Ellen felt positively bold. "Do you want to work together?" she asked Sue.

Sue smiled, her pale face suddenly flushing pink. "Yes," she said.

Ellen could see that Judy didn't want to change, especially when Chris Lambros also chose the white building. Judy had already told Ellen she thought Chris was cute. "See—'Greek Revival,' " he said, pointing to a label below the picture. "That's me." Judy shrugged at Ellen, who nodded.

Ellen and Sue talked about what they wanted to do. "We could build a model," Sue suggested. "There's a street near me where they're still building houses. The workmen always leave some pieces of siding and shingles around."

"That would be good," Ellen said.

When school was dismissed for the day and Ellen, Judy, and Louise crowded into a seat near the back of their bus, Judy turned to Ellen. "Whatever possessed you to pair up with that Sue Kitchner?"

"I wanted to do my project on a house like ours, and she was just standing there . . ." Ellen started.

"Sue Kitchner?" Louise put in. "You mean Bean Pole? She's in my math class. Never says a word to anyone but always has her answer ready whenever Howe calls on her. Creepy."

"Stuck up," Judy said.

"I don't know," Ellen said, reluctant to disagree with Judy and Louise. "She seemed okay."

"You just got here. It probably takes awhile to see what she's really like, right, Jude?" Louise said.

"Yeah," Judy said. "Anyway, I bet I know why she picked Sue. She wanted a good mark on her project for lover-boy Mitchell."

"Right," Ellen said, and laughed.

"You gotta watch out for this one. She goes for older men," Judy said to Louise. "I'm still waiting for her to tell me about her night with that cute friend. What was his name?"

"Greg," Ellen said. She had hoped Judy had forgotten about him. "But he's not a friend of mine. And nothing happened."

"Sure, sure," Judy said. She winked at Louise.

"Come on, you guys," Ellen said. "I'm serious." But she didn't protest further. She knew well enough that to Greg she was a little kid, not even worth a glance. And, no matter how many times she repeated his words, "No thanks, Ellen, I take it black," trying to read into them some hidden message of love, the sentence remained a simple request for black coffee. Still, if Judy thought he was interested in her, it made her *feel* more interesting.

The bus rattled around a corner and wheezed to a halt at their stop. They worked their way up the crowded aisle and hopped off. Judy took out a fresh pack of Juicy Fruit and handed a stick to Louise and one to Ellen. As they unwrapped the silver foil and folded the gum into their mouths, Judy said, "I almost forgot, I have a new joke. My cousin Aileen told it to me on the phone last night."

"I'll walk partway with you so I can hear it, too," Louise said.

"Okay," Judy said, crushing her gum with her front teeth before moving it to her right cheek. "Ready?" she asked. "What goes in hard and stiff and comes out soft and mushy?"

Ellen repeated the question out loud, then blushed scarlet and covered her mouth at the obvious answer. Without warning, an image of Greg naked flashed in her mind. She glanced at Louise and they both giggled. "I don't know," Ellen said at last. "What?"

"You don't know?" Judy teased. "I've been giving you people all kinds of hints. C'mon. One guess." She cracked her gum against her back teeth.

Ellen and Louise both shook their heads.

"Well, all right, then," Judy said. "It's chewing gum!" She pulled the gum from her mouth and let it fall in a snakey ribbon onto her tongue. "I can't help it if yuns have dirty minds."

Ellen laughed with a mixture of shame and relief. "That's good," she said. "Now I have one." It was now or never. She plunged in and began reciting the limerick she had memorized. "There was a young lady named Grace/Who had eyes in a very odd place/She could sit on the hole/Of a mouse or a mole/And stare the beast square in the face."

When she reached the end, instead of the embarrassed giggles that had greeted Judy's joke, there was only silence. Ellen blushed. She must have made a terrible mistake. She wished *she* could find a hole in the sidewalk, and crawl into it. Then, to her surprise, Judy let out a burst of laughter. "Oh, I get it. Don't you, Lou? You have to listen to the words. Say it again, El."

Ellen, relieved that her offering had been accepted, repeated the verse. By the time Louise turned back toward her own house at the corner of Dahlia, all three girls were reciting the limerick.

Ellen and Judy were nearing their own houses

when Ellen noticed that her father's car was parked in the Deans' driveway. "That's odd, isn't it?" she said.

Both Mr. Gerson and Mr. Dean were working the day shift this week—starting at 7:00 in the morning and ending at 3:00 in the afternoon. It was now about 2:45, so there had to be a reason for her father to be home early—and in the wrong driveway. She had a feeling it wasn't something good.

Judy opened her front door, and the two girls entered the house. The first person they saw was Mr. Gerson. He took Judy's hands and said, "Don't worry now. Your dad had an accident at work this afternoon, but he's going to be all right. The heat in the open hearth got to him, and when he passed out, he hit his head on one of the loading carts."

They could see Mr. Dean stretched out on the couch in the living room. He was a small, almost gnomelike man, a foot shorter than his wife, but with long, tightly muscled arms. His body seemed to disappear under the blanket that covered him, except for his unusually large head, which had a fat bandage on one side. His eyes were closed.

Judy tiptoed into the living room and knelt beside him, putting her arm across his chest. Mrs. Dean, who had been tucking the blanket around his feet, patted Judy lightly on the back. "Don't worry none. He just needs some rest now. You know your daddy's tough. The mines couldn't get him and the steel mill's not going to neither."

Mr. Dean opened an eye and winked at Judy.

Ellen watched the scene from the kitchen with an undefined longing. Her father's words broke into her reverie.

"He asked his foreman if he could take his break ten minutes early since he wasn't feeling well. But no, production comes before people. It's lousy Willie Dean had to suffer, but maybe this will shake people up and we can change things. The workers must have equal control with management over safety conditions. We need to organize a safety committee. . . ." Her father's face had taken on that animated, electrified look Ellen had come to dread. She didn't want Mr. Dean or anyone else getting hurt, but couldn't someone else do the fixing, the changing, the organizing?

"Why does it always have to be you?" she blurted out.

Mr. Gerson looked at her for what seemed like an eternity. Finally he said, "Then who?" The words hung in the air, unanswered.

seven

*M*r. Mitchell wanted all the class projects completed by the end of the following week. Since most of the materials the girls needed were near Sue's house, Sue suggested they work at her place. This was fine with Ellen—she didn't have to think up an excuse for *not* inviting Sue to her house, the way she did with Judy, Louise, and Sandy.

On Monday, Ellen rode home with Sue on her bus. She lived on the opposite side of the shopping center, in the Poinsettia Gate Section—12 Poppy Lane. Ellen was amazed when she first entered Sue's house. Though there wasn't much furniture, the living room was almost filled with a piano.

"It's a baby grand," Sue said, after Ellen exclaimed over its size.

"Do you know how to play it?" Ellen asked.

"Some," Sue said, heading for the kitchen. "My mom said she'd make some cookies for us. Do you want a couple?"

"Sure." Ellen sat at the kitchen table with Sue and sank her teeth into a densely packed chocolate chip cookie. She took a sip of milk. The house seemed awfully quiet. "Isn't your mother home?" Ellen asked. She thought she had the only mother who was usually off someplace.

"She's home, but she's asleep," Sue said. "She's a nurse on the night shift at Valley Hospital. Usually she gets up at five—it's supper for my dad and me and breakfast for my mom. Sometimes we even have pancakes."

Ellen laughed.

"I know it seems upside-down, but . . ." Sue crushed the remains of her cookie on her paper napkin.

"Not really," Ellen said quickly. Next to Sue's parents her own were not only upside-down but inside out and backwards. She swallowed the last of her milk. "Should we see if we can find the things we need for our model?" Ellen asked, moving to a safer topic.

Sue's father had given them a piece of plywood for a base. They scavenged enough pale yellow siding to make a good-sized model of a Fairmore Hills house. Then they cut holes for windows, taped clear cellophane over the openings for glass, and glued crossed toothpicks over the cellophane to create windowpanes.

On Wednesday Ellen rode home with Sue again, and the girls went back to the building site. This time they found a discarded, slightly warped shingle and used it to fashion a roof. Cutting it into small rectangles, they glued them together in overlapping rows that looked amazingly lifelike.

Once they had finished putting together their

model, they worked together writing the accompanying report for their oral presentation.

"I wish we could just hand it in," Sue said. "I'm terrified at the thought of standing up in front of the class."

"So am I," Ellen said.

"You? I don't believe it!" Sue said. "You jump right into everything so easily. You've only been here a few weeks and already you're best friends with the most popular girl in school."

"That's just luck," Ellen said. "Judy lives right across the street."

Sue shook her head. "It's more than luck. If I lived there instead of you, Judy wouldn't be my friend any more than she is now."

Ellen remembered Judy's comment about Sue. "Stuck up," she had said. "Maybe Judy thinks you don't want *her* for a friend," Ellen said gently.

"Maybe she's right," Sue answered back. "Judy may be pretty and popular and all that. But she seems kind of *empty* to me."

Ellen was startled into silence. She couldn't imagine anyone not wanting Judy as a friend. "But she's so nice. She really is," Ellen said. She felt a sudden rush of anger at Sue for putting her in the position of defending Judy. If anyone needed defending, Ellen thought, it was Sue. But she didn't say that. She liked Sue, and felt comfortable with her in a way she never did with Louise, Sandy—and maybe even Judy.

Ellen didn't want to pursue that thought. "Let's just drop it, okay?"

"Sure," Sue agreed. "Anyway, this isn't solving our oral report problem. I have a hard enough time saying 'here' at roll call. If I have to do an oral report, I'm sure I'll die."

"Boy, I thought I was bad," Ellen said. "Look, I'll do the oral part. You just hold up the model, all right?"

Sue nodded and flashed a radiant smile. "Thanks, Ellen," she said.

Their report was scheduled for Tuesday, right after Mary Konski and Joe Savage's. Ellen had already made three trips to the bathroom; her mouth was dry, and she felt alternately hot, then cold. Why did I ever volunteer to do this? she thought, as she entered the classroom. When she saw Sue, already sitting down, she knew why. Sue's ordinarily pale skin was bleached white. She looked as though she would have liked to shrink herself, Alice in Wonderland style, and disappear inside their model house. Ellen usually sat in the back of the room beside Judy, but today she slipped into the empty seat next to Sue. "Hey, smile," she said to Sue.

Sue gave her a fake grimace, moving only her mouth. The she let out a nervous laugh. "Sorry, Ellen. I know I'm being silly. I just hope I won't shake so much I drop the model."

"You won't. You'll be fine," Ellen assured her, not feeling at all sure. She opened her notebook to a clean sheet and began to fill the page with a single word—Donald. That was, she had recently learned, Mr. Mitchell's first name.

The bell rang and Mr. Mitchell sauntered in and took attendance. After Ellen's "Here," she sat back, willing him to look her way. He rewarded her with a glance, and Ellen smiled. Everything would go well.

Joe and Mary gave their report while Ellen alternately doodled and read through her own report. If anyone had asked her what their topic was, she couldn't have said. Teepees? Log cabins?

Then Mr. Mitchell was calling her name and Sue's, and the two of them walked to the front of the room. Ellen's two handwritten sheets of paper rattled against each other and her knees shook beneath her skirt. A voice that she didn't recognize as her own began mouthing the words she and Sue had written—with some help from the Fairmore Hills Chamber of Commerce Fact Sheet. "The model you see here is a typical Fairmore Hills house. It is built of pressed fiberboard on a concrete foundation." She took a gulp of air while Sue held up the construction.

"Looks like a box with windows to me," John Ballantine yelled out.

"Quiet, John," Mr. Mitchell said.

Ellen threw him a grateful look and continued. "Most of the men who live in Fairmore Hills work at the new Fairmore steel mill."

Sue pointed a trembling finger at their painted backdrop of smokestacks.

"Great!" John interrupted again. "All the workers get a little box to live in. Nuttin' wit' nuttin'—like in Russia."

"Russia?" Ellen had to separate herself from that word. "What do you mean?" she asked.

John sat back arrogantly. "It's like my dad says—communism is the equal distribution of poverty for everyone."

"Hey, that's good," John's friend Don Butowski said. Big and blond and loud, he usually sat in the back of the room telling dirty jokes with John.

Ellen was confused. What was John talking about? All right, maybe their model—and Fairmore Hills houses, too—looked kind of boxlike. But she loved their house on Daffodil Drive. She had to make it clear to John Ballantine and Don Butowski—and Judy and Mr. Mitchell and everyone else—that Fairmore Hills had nothing communistic about it. Otherwise, why would her parents make fun of it, the way they had that first day?

Besides, *everyone* didn't live in the little boxes. She recalled her mother's question and echoed it now. "But where do the owners live?" she asked.

"In Judy's mansion!" someone called out.

"Yeah, with Judy," another voice added, to a chorus of hooting and whistling from the boys in the room.

Ellen could see Judy in her seat at the back, enjoying the attention. That was all right with Ellen. At least she had shown that there was nothing red about Fairmore Hills.

"Okay, boys," Mr. Mitchell cut in. "Pipe down. Let's give Ellen and Sue the same consideration we would want ourselves. Go on, Ellen," he said, turning to her and nodding.

Ellen looked back at her paper to find the place

where she had left off. But before she located it, she heard Sue ask John in a surprisingly strong voice, "Did you say that communism is the equal distribution of poverty for everyone?"

"Yeah," he answered. "Wanna make something of it?"

"No, I don't want to argue, if that's what you mean." Sue's voice sounded shakier now, but she went on. "I just think that, if there has to be poverty, isn't it better that it be distributed equally, instead of some people being poor and other people rich?"

"Are you a commie or what?" John said angrily.

Sue shook her head but didn't answer.

Another voice called out "Pinko!" Instantly an impromptu chorus took up the word and began chanting, "Pinko! Pinko!"

Ellen looked around in panic. She could see Judy at the back of the room, her lips mimicking the others. Aunt Sonia had said it was hate that turned ordinary people into monsters. But Judy didn't seem to be spurred by hate. She was just going along with the crowd.

Why didn't Mr. Mitchell do something? Wasn't he going to stop them? An image of the mounted police standing before a crowd of marchers, doing nothing to stop the attackers, flashed in her mind. Shouldn't Mr. Mitchell defend Sue? After all, she had only asked a question—a good question, too.

Finally Mr. Mitchell strolled toward the front of the room and held up his arms for silence. "I'm sure

Sue isn't a pinko or a commie. Are you, Sue?" he asked.

The voice that came from Sue's lips sounded close to tears. "No," she croaked.

Ellen had an impulse to move closer and put an arm around her. Instead she took a step back. Sue was tainted.

The bell rang then and Ellen returned quickly to her seat, waiting until Sue had left the room before walking out with Judy. Behind them Ellen could hear John Ballantine exclaiming, "The only good commie's a dead commie!"

Judy turned to Ellen. "Didn't I tell you there was something weird about Sue?"

Ellen nodded.

But later, washing her face before going to bed, she confronted her eyes in the bathroom mirror. "Coward," they accused. "Traitor!"

Is it my fault Sue asked that question? What could I do? Ellen silently answered.

But the eyes continued to accuse her until her glance skittered away from their reflection, and she snapped off the light.

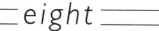

eight

There was going to be an all-school variety show on Friday evening, June 5. "Let's put an act together," Judy said to Ellen, Sandy, and Louise.

It was a Saturday afternoon. The four of them were involved in one of their favorite activities: walking around the shopping center.

"What could we do?" Sandy said

"Yes, what?" Louise echoed.

"I can't think of everything. What about you guys?" Judy said.

They were just passing the pet shop window when Judy stopped abruptly. "I know! Ellen can sing 'How much is that doggie in the window,' and the rest of us can . . . can . . ."

". . . can dress up like dogs and dance around," Sandy finished.

"Oh, no," Ellen said. "I'm not getting up onstage and singing all by myself."

"I'll sing with you," Louise said. "I'm not too good, but I'm loud. Those two can be the dogs."

"Okay," Judy said. She thought a moment, then

added, "I have an even better idea. Sandy and I together could be one huge dog. She'll be the front end and I'll be the back."

"You already have the waggly tail," Ellen said.

"Hey, watch it," Judy said. "You're gonna get your own tail swatted." She raised her hand as if to spank her, and Ellen darted away, running behind Sandy. Giggling and shrieking, they moved away from the pet shop window.

They decided to call themselves "The Petshop Quartet." Making that decision was easy. Designing the dog costume was going to be hard, but luckily Louise's mother had a sewing machine. The girls trooped over to Louise's house to talk to Mrs. Warski. She said she would help sew the costume once the girls knew what they wanted.

Sandy thought they should make the full costume of fur, cutting holes only for the eyes. "I saw some material in Lobel's that would be perfect," she said.

"Perfect for who? We're gonna die from heat frustration inside a costume like that. And anyway," Judy went on, "who has the money to pay for all that material?"

No one answered.

Ellen said, "Maybe we could make the costume with holes to stick the legs through. If we could get some worn sheets, dye them, sew on ears and a tail . . ."

"That sounds good," Louise said. She stood up. "Wait," she told them and ran into her room, returning a couple of minutes later with a fluffy blue slipper on each hand. "Don't they look just like paws?"

"Sure," Judy said. "Paws are always blue."

"Oh, you know what I mean. I think they'll be cute," Louise said.

"Maybe," Judy conceded. "But dogs have four legs. If we're gonna use slippers, we're gonna need another pair."

"Someone must have a pair of slippers like these. Let's ask around," Louise said.

They met at Louise's again the next day. Judy and Ellen had each brought a worn sheet. Sandy was apologetic. When they moved to Fairmore Hills, she said, her mother had insisted on new sheets and towels, even if the family had to go hungry for a week. "And that's just about what we did," Sandy said. "But now there's not one old sheet in the house." She did bring a pair of soft brown socks, though, just right for two floppy ears.

They set to work, draping, cutting, pinning, and basting. A girl in Sandy's science class loaned them a pair of slippers that were made of the same furlike fabric as Louise's, except that they were white. "Same difference," Judy said, approving them. "Lots of dogs have different-colored paws."

On the following Saturday they made another trip to the shopping center, this time for a package of Rit dye. They chose Chocolate Brown for the most doggy look. But when they dunked their already yellowed sheets in the brown dye bath, the fabric turned an uneven, slightly greenish mud color. "It's all right," Judy pronounced. "Dogs can be any color." When they had done the final stitching, Judy stepped into her end and switched her tail—a terry cloth belt borrowed from Louise's father's bathrobe. Sandy stepped into her end and wagged her sock ears. The four costume-makers were thrilled with the result.

During this time Ellen hardly saw her family. On the afternoons when they worked on the costume at Louise's house, she dropped her books at home, announced where she was going and when she'd return, and left. Sometimes the house was empty and there would be a note for her on the kitchen table: "Dear El, Had to run to Nora's for emergency meeting. Mikey and I'll be back at 6:00. Love, Mom." "Dear El, Please put chicken in oven at 5:00. Working on new appeal. Love, Mom." Her father, it was true, was home more often in the evenings now. But he usually spent them at the kitchen table with a group of men from the mill—the new safety committee. They would talk long and loud into the night, as the table became a clutter of cigarette-butt-filled ashtrays and empty beer cans.

Ellen told her parents that she and her friends were going to perform in the school show. "We'll have to come and see our star," Mrs. Gerson said.

"Definitely," Mr. Gerson agreed. "When is it?" He printed "Ellen's Show" across the June 5 box on the wall calendar.

The longing for her parents' attention tugged at her. She drew back. They'll probably forget anyway, she told herself. But the strong black lines that her father had used to mark the calendar made her hope against her will.

On Monday morning, halfway through hygiene, Ellen heard the familiar squawk of the public address system. She braced herself for the wail of the air raid siren. But instead there was a tap, tap of fingernails against microphone and a whoosh of amplified breath. "This is Mrs. Whiteside," the voice of the music teacher said. "All students performing in the variety show should come to the auditorium at three."

Ellen shivered. She had spent so much time, thought, and energy making the costume that she had more or less forgotten her part—the singing. Now the reality hit her. She was actually going to have to walk out onstage and sing! How did she get into this? More to the point, how could she get out?

She spent the rest of the morning concocting reasons for leaving the show. "I broke my toe/arm/nose/wrist/glasses." "My aunt/cousin/parakeet/sister/dog died." When she ran out of body parts to break (and remembered that she didn't wear glasses), when she had killed off every imaginary relative (and remembered that she didn't have a parakeet or a dog), she knew she was trapped.

"I'm so nervous," she confided to Louise and Sandy when they met at lunchtime.

"Me, too," Louise echoed.

"What are you two nervous about?" Sandy said. "Today's meeting is just a rehearsal."

"That's easy for you to say," Ellen pointed out.

"You and Judy are going to be hidden inside the dog costume. Louise and I don't have anything to hide behind."

"Do you want to trade?" Sandy asked. She almost sounded serious. In fact, Ellen realized, she *did* sound serious. She wondered if secretly Sandy had wanted to be one of the singers all along.

Ellen had a chance to escape, to hide inside the costume. But the answer to Sandy's question, she decided, was no. She didn't want to trade. Maybe her hands would be clammy and her stomach jittery, but she wanted to sing the song. "That's okay, Sandy. I may die of stage fright, but at least I'll die trying."

Louise draped an arm around Ellen's shoulders. "Ellen wouldn't leave me. She's no coward," she said.

It was so wonderful to be part of this group. But she had a sudden image of Sue, her head bent against the taunts that no one—certainly not Ellen—had protested. She shook her head to dispel the image. I am a coward though, Ellen thought.

The rehearsal wasn't nearly as scary as Ellen had imagined it would be. Their act was the fourth on the program. First Kevin Connolly played "America the Beautiful" on the accordion; then the Stinson twins, Mary and Martha, did a tap dance. Faith Auerbach was third. She stood in the middle of the stage and talked about how peanut butter stuck to the roof of her mouth. It was hard to understand what she was saying, but Ellen wasn't sure if that was because she herself was getting nervous—their act was next—or because Faith really *did* have peanut butter stuck to the roof of her mouth.

Then Mrs. Whiteside looked up from her clipboard and called, "Petshop Quartet, are you here?"

Judy and Sandy didn't have the costume with them, so Ellen and Louise walked out by themselves. Mrs. Whiteside struck the opening piano chords and, facing the empty auditorium, the two girls sang their song. When they reached the end they walked off, leaning into each other and giggling.

"That was so awful," Louise said.

"I just know I'm going to die," Ellen moaned. She felt wonderful.

Sue Kitchner was among those waiting to perform. Ellen acted as though she hadn't seen her, as though Sue were invisible. It was the way she had behaved toward Sue ever since the day of their report. It was easy: if Sue were invisible Ellen wasn't really *avoiding* her; she just wasn't there. The technique worked better in social studies than here in the auditorium. Ellen couldn't help wondering what Sue was going to do in the show.

Standing alone, Sue was a painful reminder to Ellen. She looks so alone, Ellen thought. And she wouldn't be, if I hadn't dropped her. But then what would have happened to me? I wouldn't be sitting here with Louise, Judy, and Sandy.

Ellen was anxious to get away now. She turned to her friends and said, "We don't have to stay for the whole program, do we? Let's go."

"Yeah," Judy said. "The best part is over anyway."

Whispering and laughing together, the four left in a group.

The next few days zipped by, a blur of school, meals, homework, and lots of rehearsals. Almost every evening there was an emergency phone call from one of her friends, checking on one detail or another.

Then it was Friday. Ellen awoke even earlier than she had the first day of school, and as on the first day, she couldn't eat breakfast. But her nervousness today was of a different sort. She felt jumpy, tingly, excited. She lifted Mikey high and swung him around till the room spun and he shrieked with delight. Setting him down she said, "You're going to come see me onstage, aren't you?" She could ask him the question and get her parents' answer without seeming to want it.

"Sure, we'll all be there," Mrs. Gerson said. "Eight o'clock?"

"Yes," Ellen repeated. "Eight o'clock."

Louise's mother had invited the four girls for supper. They would go directly there after school for one final rehearsal before the performance.

The school day seemed interminable. Ellen had discovered that all the school clocks were like the one in study hall, and she spent most of each class watching the big hand on the clock, willing it to make its two-minute leap. But when the dismissal bell finally rang at 3:20, and Ellen went to meet her friends at the bus boarding area, she wished she could have that lost time back. Just four hours and forty minutes to go, she thought.

When they got to Louise's, the first thing they did was to check out the costume. It was in three parts—a front end, a back end, and a head, all connected with rows of hooks and eyes. Judy stepped into the back end and bent at the waist, holding on to Sandy in the front end. The dog's head that Sandy wore had eye holes for Sandy, but Judy was sightless inside the costume and had to depend on Sandy to lead her. Ellen and Louise hooked up all the closures, and all four went through their performance one last time.

Supper was hot dogs and baked beans. Judy spooned a hefty helping of beans onto her plate and passed the serving dish past Sandy to Louise. "No beans for Sandy," she said. "It's hard enough to breathe inside that costume."

"But it's all right for you?" Louise said sarcastically.

"Well, sure," Judy said. "I'm the tail." She started to sing. "Beans, beans, good for your heart, the more you eat, the more you . . ."

"Um, girls," Louise's mother interrupted. "Don't you think we could find another topic for the dinner table?"

"I don't know, Mrs. Warski," Sandy said, laughing. "It's pretty hard with Judy around."

By the time supper was finished and the dishes cleared away, it was 6:30. They had to be at the school in one hour. Ellen and Louise changed into their performance clothes—poodle skirts (Louise wore Judy's), short-sleeved white blouses, white bobby sox, and their brown-and-white saddle shoes. Then Judy, the makeup expert, took over. First Louise, then Ellen sat still while Judy applied powder, blush, mascara, and lipstick. Ellen looked at the finished product, barely recognizing the painted face that mirrored her gaze through eyes made huge with black liner.

Was that really her—Ellen Gerson—under that mask? Ellen had a sudden vision of herself onstage, her makeup cracking like old plaster and dropping off in clumps, leaving her exposed—a fraud. She shook her head. No. This really is me, she told herself.

At 7:15, with the dog costume bundled in a grocery bag, they squeezed into the backseat of the Warskis' car. Mr. and Mrs. Warski sat in front, along with Louise's grandmother, who had come by bus from Pittsburgh that morning especially to see her granddaughter's performance. Louise's parents seemed as nervous and excited as the girls. Every few minutes Mr. Warski would tell one of the girls to "break a leg." When he pulled in to the circular drive in front of the school and they climbed out of the car, he called to them, "Remember, girls . . ."

They answered him in chorus. "Break a leg!" Shaking their heads and laughing, they pulled open the front door.

Almost before there was time to think, Ellen and her friends were in the wings listening as Faith Auerbach mumbled on about peanut butter on the roof of her mouth. Then she wasn't talking anymore and there was the sound of clapping. The curtain closed.

"You're on, girls," Mrs. Whiteside said. She strode to the piano. Judy and Sandy, walking as one inside the costume, positioned themselves on stage. Mrs. Whiteside played the first notes of the song and the curtain opened on the sock-eared, terry-cloth-tailed, slipper-pawed dog. An outpouring of laughter rose from the audience. Mrs. Whiteside continued playing while Judy and Sandy swayed to the music. She would play it once all the way through before Ellen and Louise came onstage.

The end of the song was approaching. The laughing had died. Mrs. Whiteside looked back at Ellen and Louise. Louise tugged at Ellen's arm, but Ellen pulled back. "I can't remember the words!" she whispered in panic.

"Come on!" Mrs. Whiteside mouthed and, as she was about to hit the piano keys, beginning the song again, Louise yanked Ellen onstage.

Then, somehow, they were going through their practiced motions—hugging the dog and stroking its ears—and, by some miracle, Ellen was singing with Louise, one note following the other almost as if she knew what she was singing.

It was over. Sandy lifted off the dog head and unhooked the front end of the costume from the back to reveal Judy, blinking in the spotlight. Another rush of laughter rose from the audience. They all joined hands and bowed.

Ellen stood onstage between Louise and Sandy, her mouth stretched and lifted in an absurdly wide grin. She was sure she had never heard any sound as lovely as the waterfall of clapping. Louise was pulling her toward the wings.

"First we can't get her onstage and now we can't get her off," she said.

"You're too much, El," Sandy said.

"Yeah," Judy said. "But we'll keep her around a little longer anyway." She gave Ellen's shoulder a light punch that warmed Ellen like a caress.

Ellen was still grinning when she and her friends entered the auditorium from a side door to join their families for the rest of the program. After the glare of the spotlit stage it took awhile to adjust to the darkness of the auditorium, but within a few moments Louise, Sandy, and Judy spotted their parents.

They're not here, Ellen told herself, raking the rows front to back. I knew it all along. Why did I let myself think otherwise? Stupid, stupid. I should know by now not to count on them!

Her eyes brimmed with tears. Angry with herself, she swiped at them with the back of her hand. Several people seemed to be waving at her from the other end of the auditorium. It was Mr. and Mrs. Dean, Judy . . . and Mikey. Yes, there he was, bouncing on Mrs. Dean's leg. She waved back at them, then made her way around the perimeter of the auditorium to join them.

Mrs. Dean took her hands. "Your folks came by earlier and asked if we'd mind Mikey. They was real upset and had to rush off. I think a friend is in the hospital—they said something about a life or death situation."

"Oh," Ellen said. Life or death. The Rosenbergs. Again. A thought leaped across her mind. I wish they would die! She regretted it instantly and bit her lip, as if to take it back. She sat in the empty seat beside Mrs. Dean. Mikey climbed into her lap. "Did you see me, Mikey? Onstage?"

"Doggie in da window, doggie in da window," Mikey sang at full volume, rocking back against her.

Ellen put a finger to her lips. "Sshhh," she whispered, smiling now.

Beth Haas and Kathleen Shaunessey had come out onstage. Beth, wearing a long dress, sat down at the piano and began to play *dah dah dah dah dah dah*— two-fingered chopsticks! Kathleen hovered beside her, turning the sheets of music at each *dah*. It was ridiculous, making a big production over nothing, but when Beth and Kathleen took their bows, the room exploded with laughter and applause.

The curtain closed. When it reopened Sue Kitchner was seated at the piano. Ellen had never stayed for Sue's rehearsals. Now she scanned the mimeographed program until she came to Sue's name, followed by the words "J. S. Bach, Goldberg Variations, Nos. 1-3."

She looked up at Sue's taut profile and hands with their long, fine-boned fingers. Ellen felt a rush of sympathy for her and tensed involuntarily. Then Sue lowered her fingers to the keys and started to play.

Softly, gently, the melody floated out. The music quickened. Sue's fingers flew over the keys and the notes merged and separated, high notes dancing away, then returning.

Ellen saw a different Sue now. Her pale skin was dramatic in contrast to her dark hair, which she had pulled back and tied with a ribbon at the base of her neck. Bent close to the keyboard, fierce in concentration, she looked—what was the word?—radiant. She seemed to glow from within, the way Ellen's father did when he spoke with passion about bosses' wrongs, workers' rights. Both her father and Sue were carried away by a force greater than themselves. That had never happened to Ellen. Maybe it never would, she thought. She didn't pity Sue anymore; she envied her.

The music ended. Sue stood up, tucking her chin toward her chest in a shy bow. She walked offstage quickly to a smattering of polite applause.

"At last, *that's* over," Judy hissed to Ellen.

Ellen nodded, relieved only that the auditorium was unlit so no one could see her shame-reddened face.

nine

*I*t was very crowded in the Deans' kitchen with Sandy and Sandy's parents, brother, and sister; Louise, her parents and grandmother; Ellen and Mikey; and all the Deans in a crush around the table. "It's a good thing your folks couldn't make it," Mr. Dean said. "I don't see where we coulda squeezed one more soul in here."

"What a thing to say!" Mrs. Dean chided, towering over her husband, her hands on her hips. "Doesn't Ellen feel bad enough that her parents couldn't come without your rubbing it in."

"You know I was only joking, Mother," Mr. Dean said. "I'm sorry they're not here, too."

Ellen accepted the dish of ice cream Mrs. Dean handed her. She smiled. "Thank you." She, for one, was glad her parents hadn't come. She could just see it: with all these people, her mother would be passing around a petition and her father would be organizing a union meeting.

Mrs. Warski turned to Ellen. "I hope everything's all right. I mean, you didn't have a death in your family or anything, did you?"

"Oh, no, nothing like that," Ellen was quick to answer. But what explanation could she give? She stared at her slice of vanilla, chocolate, and strawberry ice cream, whose edges were beginning to merge as they melted. Should she just repeat what Mrs. Dean had told her—that someone was in the hospital? The trouble was, Ellen had a hard time lying. Whenever she said something that wasn't strictly true, she stumbled over the words, her face reddened, and—worst of all—her mouth turned up in a grin, announcing that she was just kidding. It would be pretty dumb to grin about someone being in the hospital. She stirred her dish of ice cream till it became a pinkish brown soup.

Mrs. Dean spoke. "Her folks had to go to New York City. A close friend of theirs is sick. Mrs. Gerson said it was life or death."

Ellen was grateful that Mrs. Dean had answered for her. But there were those words again: *life or death.* They made an instant link for her with the Rosenbergs. Could they have triggered the same response in Mikey? What else could have made him suddenly begin to singsong, "Rosy bugs, rosy bugs. Free the rosy bugs"?

"What bugs?" Mrs. Dean said. She picked Mikey up and hugged him. "You little devil. Are you telling these folks I have bugs in my house?"

Mikey laughed in delight. "Rosy bugs, rosy bugs..." he sang even louder.

Ellen glanced at the faces around the table. Was it possible they didn't know what he was really saying? Didn't they pay any attention to what was happening in the world? Ellen felt just a shade superior to her friends and their parents. How can they be so dumb? she wondered. She immediately pushed the thought away and looked at Judy, Louise, and Sandy, each so pretty and fun loving. She felt, once again, incredibly, amazingly, astoundingly lucky to be part of their circle.

It was almost eleven when Ellen took Mikey back to their still-empty house. After two tackles, she had finally succeeded in getting one of Mikey's legs into his pajamas, when they heard the familiar rattle of their car as it pulled into the driveway. Mikey slithered out of Ellen's grasp and ran, trailing his pajama leg, for the door. It creaked open and her parents came in, looking weary but pleased. Mr. Gerson lifted Mikey and swung him high. Mrs. Gerson caught Ellen around the waist and whirled her once around. "Good news," she said. "It looks as if they may reopen the case."

Her mother went into great detail describing lawyers' appeals, judges' decisions, as if Ellen were as interested as she. She wasn't. "You missed my show," Ellen said.

"Oh, Hon, that's right. We're so sorry we couldn't see your skit," Mrs. Gerson said. "I hope you can understand."

"I understand, all right," Ellen said bitterly.

Now Mr. Gerson spoke. "You know there are two innocent lives hanging in the balance now. We're trying to tip the scales on the side of justice."

Ellen hated that sort of talk—it sounded as if it came right off one of those fliers handed out at demonstrations. She could see the thick black ink, each phrase punctuated with an exclamation point.

TWO LIVES HANG IN THE BALANCE!
JOIN US!
TIP THE SCALES ON THE SIDE OF JUSTICE!

Maybe her friends and their parents were better off not caring about the Rosenbergs at all. Holding on to that thought, she said good-night.

On Monday morning, as Ellen was hurrying from homeroom to English, a tall boy she didn't know nodded to her in passing. "You were good," he said.

She looked behind her. There was no one there. Was he talking to her? She shrugged. He must think I'm someone else, she decided.

Before she got to English, though, two more unknown people had spoken to her. "Hey," one girl said, grabbing her by the wrist and nearly swinging her around. "You're the one that sang 'Doggie in the Window.' " Her tone made it sound as though she were accusing Ellen of a crime. The girl was at least six inches taller and thirty pounds heavier than Ellen, and Ellen hesitated before admitting her guilt.

"Yes," she whispered.

The girl released Ellen's wrist. "You have a real nice voice," she announced.

Ellen wasn't going to argue. "Thanks," she said.

Then, from across the corridor, someone else called to her, "Nice going."

I guess our act really did make a hit! she thought.

She pulled open the door of English class. Several people burst into applause, and someone called, "Encore, encore!"

Ellen felt her face grow hot. *I must look like a tomato,* she thought. But her blush this morning was one of deep pleasure. She covered her face with her hands, pretending a modesty she didn't quite feel, and slid into her seat.

By the end of the day she had gotten so used to the congratulations and pats on the back from classmates, the nods and smiles from people she didn't even know, that when her performance was ignored, she found herself fishing for compliments. "Did you go to the show on Friday?" she asked Kathy Bienke, who sat behind her in science.

"No, I forgot about it."

"Oh," Ellen said. She felt slighted.

When Patti Reilly, who had the locker next to hers in gym, didn't say anything either, Ellen was hurt. She knew Patti was there because she had seen her in the audience. Now she couldn't restrain herself from asking, "What did you think of the variety show?"

"It was all right," Patti said. "But it got kind of boring in the middle."

Was she including their act? Ellen stopped asking questions. She wanted to hear only good things.

With just two more weeks of school before summer vacation, there was a feeling that whatever the students were supposed to learn had already been taught, and if it hadn't, well, there was always next year. Homework assignments dwindled and classes were heavy on audiovisuals. In English they watched the movie *The Yearling* spread over three classes. By the final day, Ellen's eyes were so red from crying, she thought they must be permanently bloodshot. It was all right, though. Everyone else's eyes were red, too—even John Ballantine's. In hygiene they watched an animated short film called "Pretty Is as Pretty Does," about the merits of smiling. And in science they saw a film about milking machines, which seemed to have no connection at all to anything else.

But if no one was much interested in studying, there was something else that drew everyone to school: a spate of contests—to choose the best athlete, the best scholar, the handsomest boy, the prettiest girl. Ellen, who had only been at Fairmore for two months, didn't feel she knew enough of the students to vote. But then Mr. Slavin announced a final contest. Every teacher and every student could cast his or her vote to choose Miss Fairmore Hills Junior High School. "Remember," he said, "this is not just a beauty contest. The winner should be chosen for her grades, her talent, and her contribution to the school."

When the nominating ballots were distributed in homeroom the next day, Ellen didn't hesitate before entering her choice: Judy Dean.

Ellen just knew Judy would win, and the thought that the future Miss Fairmore Hills Junior High School was her very best friend made her giddy with happiness.

On Friday morning, when the names of the four finalists were posted, Ellen checked the list just to make sure Judy's name was there. It was. Satisfied, she started to walk away, then stopped. Some trick of the eye had made her think, for a moment, that she had seen her own name printed there. She turned back. Two other people were reading the list. She waited for them to leave. Now that her own name was the one she was looking for, she didn't want to appear too interested. She sidled past the bulletin board and cast a furtive glance at the list. Yes. There it was: Ellen Karla Gerson, typed in right between Maybell Ferguson and Debra McSparran.

She drifted away in a blissful daze. Me, she thought, a finalist for Miss Fairmore Hills Junior High. The title had seemed so beyond her grasp that she had never dreamed of reaching for it. And now . . . now . . .

Ellen floated through the day with a crazy smile glued to her face. Every so often, in the middle of something else — waiting for her word in a spelling bee, changing into her uniform in gym, writing a math problem on the board — she would think, Me. A finalist! Without warning, a bubble of joy would percolate up and spill over in a laugh. She thanked her lucky stars over and over that she'd gone ahead with the talent show, and especially that she hadn't hidden inside the dog costume. That was what had made everyone notice her. Could anyone possibly be happier than she?

Even the air raid siren that shattered the silence of

study hall couldn't pierce her euphoria. She hugged her knees and pressed her head against them, letting Mr. Slavin's harangue wash over her without giving it a thought—she had other, more pleasant things to think about.

Louise and Judy were already waiting to board the bus at the end of the school day when Ellen joined the line. "Hey, nice going," Judy said to her.

"Same to you," she answered. But for the first time since seeing her name on the list, Ellen felt a twinge of unease. She would, she realized, be competing with Judy. She felt she needed to explain, to excuse herself to Judy. "I couldn't believe it when I saw my name there," she said.

"I'm so happy for you," Judy said. She gave Ellen a cuff on the back that was just a touch too hard to feel good.

Louise folded her arms and pouted. "Whoever wins, you two are going to be too stuck up to associate with plain old me," she said.

"That's silly," Judy said. "Anyway, Debra Mc-Sparran is gonna win. She has all that blond hair and those baby blue eyes. That's what people like."

The bus pulled into the parking lot and they got on, squeezing into one seat together near the back.

"Well, I'm just so amazed that I was nominated. I feel like doing cartwheels—if only I knew how," Ellen said.

"Oh, I'm getting tired of all these contests," Judy said. "Anyway, I've been thinking about something more exciting." She stopped, waiting for someone to prompt her with a "What?"

Ellen was hurt by Judy's professed boredom. It made her own excitement about the contest seem silly. She couldn't help it—she was elated about being nominated. More than anything, though, she wanted Judy's friendship. "What?" she asked.

"We should have a party. Next Friday. It can be at my house. We'll invite everyone—at least everyone who matters. It will be an end-of-school blast."

"It sounds great," Louise said. "Will your folks let you?"

"Why not?" Judy said. "I have it all figured out. The party will be the nineteenth—a week before school ends. That way, in case my report card isn't too great, my parents won't be able to tell me I can't have a party—it will be over. See?" She tapped the side of her head with a forefinger.

Ellen laughed. "You're always thinking, aren't you?"

"About *some* things anyway," Louise said. She rolled her eyes across the aisle, where Larry Matthews and Julio Rosa were sitting. They all laughed.

Judy was the first one to get serious again. "C'mon, listen, you guys," she said. "If we're gonna have a party, we have a lot of planning to do. We have to decide who's coming, what we're gonna eat . . . all sorts of things. Let's meet at my house later so we can get started."

"Okay." "Sure," Louise and Ellen both agreed.

The bus pulled up to their stop. They got off. "I've got to stop at home first, but I'll be over in a little while," Louise said. She started off in the direction of her house. Judy and Ellen headed in the other direction.

They walked the last blocks together without talking. Ellen was glad for the silence. She wanted a chance to savor the thrill of the nomination and now, on top of it, the thrilling idea of Judy's party. She practically danced her way home, skipping and turning along the sidewalk.

When they reached their houses, Judy started up her driveway. "About half an hour, then?" she said, looking back at Ellen.

Ellen, not trusting ordinary words to come from her mouth, nodded and waved. She sailed up her own driveway and pulled open her door.

Mrs. Gerson, in a pose unusual for her, was standing at the kitchen counter, breaking string beans into a pot. Ellen dropped her books on the table, grabbed her mother around the waist, and whirled her around, the way her mother had done to her last week. Now her words tumbled out in a rush. "It's so amazing! I can't believe it! I was nominated for Miss Fairmore Hills Junior High and, guess what! Judy's having a party! On Friday. I have to help her plan for it. Isn't it all just too good to be true!" Out of breath, she plopped down in a chair.

"That really is wonderful, El." Her mother smiled back at her.

Well, that's good enough, Ellen thought. She fixed herself a snack of tuna fish on saltines, then headed out the door again. Judy was waiting.

ten

Planning for The Party—that was the new focus of Ellen's life. It required vast amounts of time and energy to do properly. It wasn't just a matter of deciding whom to invite, what to serve, and what games to play. That was easy. The hard part was deciding how to fix their hair and what makeup and clothes to wear.

After school each day, Ellen, Sandy, Louise, and Judy took turns in front of Judy's full-length mirror, trying on various combinations of their own and each other's clothes until they had exhausted every possibility. On Wednesday Sandy arrived with a magazine called *Crowning Glory*. Each page pictured a beautiful woman showing off her hairstyle, front view and back. Below each photograph was a diagram of a head, sectioned off in patterns of pin curls that would achieve the pictured hairdo. They flipped through the book, folding back the corners on the pages of all the hairdos they wanted to try—fourteen in all.

Judy dumped her supply of bobby pins on her vanity table and set to work. Louise wanted to try the Gamin, a cap of tight curls. Carefully following the diagram, Judy set the fifty-eight required pin curls. She lacquered Louise's head with hair spray, spun her chair around, and called, "Next!"

Sandy asked for the Poodle, a fluff of curly bangs in front and a high ponytail in back. When Judy finished setting all the curls in the Poodle diagram, there were no bobby pins left to set Ellen's hair in the Grecian Goddess style she had chosen. So, while they waited for Louise and Sandy's hair to set, Judy tried out some of her makeup techniques on Ellen's face.

Ellen was happy to have Judy experiment on her. But then Judy announced, "First I have to curl your eyelashes, El."

"Do you have to?" Ellen said. She had watched Judy curl her own eyelashes countless times, but up to now, Ellen had always come up with some excuse to avoid having hers curled. What if her eyelid got squeezed along with her lashes? The thought made her cringe.

But Judy said, "Yeah, I have to," and advanced on Ellen, eyelash curler in hand. With Louise and Sandy watching, Ellen felt powerless to resist. Judy placed the curler over Ellen's lashes and, holding the curved metal flush against her eyelid, pressed the pincers together. Hard. Ellen's eyes watered. She had an urge to blink, but she resisted, afraid that if she did, her lashes would pull out.

At last Judy released her pressure on the scissorslike grips and pulled the curler away from Ellen's eye. "Whew," Ellen breathed out in relief. Then she had to go through the procedure all over again on her other eye.

When the makeup-hairstyling session was over for the day, Ellen's hair was piled high on her head and her forehead and cheeks were edged with spitcurls. Her eyes were outlined in black pencil and her lashes crimped so tightly that the ends brushed her lids.

"You look at least seventeen!" Louise said.

That was the highest compliment Ellen could imagine. "Do I really?" She smiled broadly.

"Well, maybe sixteen," Judy granted. "But don't smile like that. The foundation will crease."

"Oh." Ellen pulled the corners of her mouth down and shook her head.

"No shaking," Judy warned. "Your curls will come loose."

"Right," Ellen said, freezing in position. "Well, see you guys tomorrow," she said. She kept her head as immobile as possible as she crossed the street.

Her mother's only comment when she came in was, "That's quite a hairdo."

Ellen didn't know whether that meant her mother liked it or not; she didn't ask. "I'm wearing it like this to Judy's party on Friday," she said.

When her father came home, his eyes widened when he saw her. He was about to say something, but the phone rang. He talked for a long time, and when he hung up at last he seemed to have forgotten about Ellen.

Mikey, though, was intrigued with her new look.

He climbed up on the chair next to hers and began patting her head all over.

"Careful, Mikey. Don't mess up my hairdo," she said. She reached up and touched something shell-like and slightly sticky. "Ugh!" she cried, and jerked her hand away, thinking something must have spilled on her hair. Then she realized that what she was feeling was her own hair-sprayed head. Oh, well, she thought, tapping the hardened surface on her way to the shower, at least I don't have to worry about my hair getting mussed.

When she came home from school on Thursday the house was empty; there was a note on the kitchen table. "Good news. Justice Douglas granted a stay. Had to go mimeograph some press releases. Be back early eve. Love, Mom." Ellen scanned the words. She didn't know exactly who Justice Douglas was, except that he was someone important. And she didn't know exactly what a stay was, except that it was something good. But she had no doubt about the subject of the note: the Rosenbergs. She crumpled the scrap of notepaper, tossed it into the trash, and left for Judy's.

That evening, though, there was a pleasantly relaxed atmosphere in the Gerson living room. After supper her parents sat together on the couch, chatting, their favorite records on the phonograph.

"At the very least," her mother said, "we've bought some time. The court won't reconvene until the fall."

"God. The relief is so great I can almost taste it," her father said.

"That's my Jess," her mother answered, "always thinking about food."

Ellen was sitting on the rug, intently pushing her cuticles back the way Judy had shown her. She couldn't help smiling. It had been a long time since she had heard her parents talk so lightly.

Just as she had done on the day of the performance, Ellen began a countdown to the party the moment she woke up the next day. When school let out, she went straight to Judy's. The big event was five hours away. There was still lots to do.

Mr. Dean had a friend at the mill whose brother ran a grocery store. He was going to let them have a case of Coke at a discount. Mrs. Dean drove them to the store to pick it up. Then they stopped at the Amoco station, which had a coin-operated ice machine, and got two bags. Back at Judy's again, they prepared the snacks they had chosen from *Family Circle*'s "Easy Party Favorites"—a package of Velveeta cut into bite-size cubes, each cube skewered with a thin pretzel stick, and bologna slices wrapped around miniature sweet gherkins. By the time they had finished arranging the snacks on Mrs. Dean's Thanksgiving platter, the painted turkey was completely covered. It was almost five o'clock.

"What about my hair?" Ellen wailed. "We only have three more hours!"

"There's time yet," Judy said calmly. "I'll set it now and do your makeup. When you come back after supper I'll brush it out."

It was close to six when Ellen crossed the street to her own house. Following Judy's warnings she tried to move as little as possible so as not to smear her makeup or disturb her set. But it was hard to keep still. Just two more hours! She was jumpy with excitement.

She pulled open her screen door and stepped inside. That was when it hit her—a grim feeling in the air, so tangible that she had an urge to lift it from her face like a clinging spider's web. She wanted to turn around and walk out.

Instead she tiptoed into the kitchen. Mrs. Gerson, her face bleached white, huddled at the table. She looked up at Ellen, and her gaze, usually so direct and clear, wavered. She looked helpless and confused, like a small child who'd just been slapped in the face and didn't know why. When she spoke her voice was almost toneless. "They're going to die tonight."

Her mother's words struck her like a blow. Their meaning was instantly clear, but Ellen couldn't believe it. "What?"

Her mother spoke slowly and deliberately, as though trying to make sense of the words herself. "The Supreme Court met in emergency session today. They overturned Justice Douglas's stay. The executions are set for eleven tonight."

The air seemed to shimmer in front of Ellen's eyes. She gripped the edge of the table, then slid into a chair opposite her mother. *I wish they would die.* The words haunted her. She had said them, thought them, just a short time ago. And now . . . "I didn't mean it!" Ellen gasped, her voice cracking as it rose.

"What?" her mother said, directing her eyes to Ellen's face.

"I didn't want them to die. I said I did. But I didn't mean it. I didn't!" Ellen begged for understanding.

She had known that the Rosenbergs had been given the death sentence. But the possibility that the sentence might one day be carried out had never seemed real. It was true that she didn't care about the Rosenbergs the way her parents did—whether they were innocent or guilty or something in-between. But she had seen their pictures, their children's pictures, so often. . . .

"I didn't want them to die," she said again.

Her mother looked past her. "Of course you didn't," she said mechanically. She clicked on the radio and began turning the knob randomly past blurted half-words and snatches of music.

Mikey came over to Ellen and climbed onto her lap. She put her arms around him and pressed her face into his back. She could feel his strong, quick heartbeat.

She closed her eyes and held him tight. He pushed her away. "Want cookie," he said.

"Not now," Ellen said automatically. "It's almost time for supper."

"Oh, God. Supper," her mother said. "I guess I

should think about putting some food on the table."
She stopped fiddling with the radio, walked over to the
food cabinet, and reached for the nearest box. "Macaroni and cheese," she announced. She took out the big
aluminum pot and filled it with water.

Left alone at the table, Ellen began toying with the
radio dial. She stopped suddenly at the words,
". . . the Court in its compassion will not carry out the
death sentences during the Jewish sabbath, which be-
gins officially at sunset—eight forty-eight this
evening."

Her mother whirled and ran back to the table. She
turned up the volume, a glint of hope in her eyes.

"Instead," the radio voice continued, "the executions of Julius and Ethel Rosenberg have been advanced to eight P.M."

Her mother closed her eyes and swallowed. "Compassion," she echoed.

Neither Ellen nor Mrs. Gerson had heard the car
drive up, but her father appeared in the doorway now, a
slumped figure in sweat-stained clothes. Mikey ran to
him and Mr. Gerson, kneeling down, wrapped his arms
around him and pressed his face into the small, sturdy
body, the same way Ellen had. Mikey never liked to be
held. He pushed his father away, too.

Ellen noted each action as though she were watching a movie rolling out frame by frame in front of her.
When she looked at the clock, the time, 6:15, had a
new reference. One hour and forty-five minutes until
the execution.

Mrs. Gerson dumped the pasta into the boiling water. Ellen set out plates, napkins, forks, glasses. When the macaroni and cheese was done, they ate. No one said much. If the radio announcer hadn't kept up a steady patter, the room would have been almost totally silent. Supper was over; Mikey got down from his chair and wandered down the hall toward his room. But Ellen and her parents clung to the table, as though to an anchor. Seven o'clock. One more hour.

Disembodied voices continued to pour from the radio. Eddie Fisher sang "Oh, my papa, to me he was so wonderful . . ." There was an advertisement for Carter's Little Liver Pills, another for Westmore, Makeup of the Stars. There was a report about the coronation of Queen Elizabeth and another about some men who had just climbed to the top of a mountain named Everest. And every few minutes the radio voice would pick up the story of Julius and Ethel Rosenberg. "The rabbi of Sing Sing prison spent several minutes with each of the condemned. . . ." "The witnesses have taken their positions in the viewing area. . . ."

Seven-thirty. Half an hour to go. Now was the time for the king's messenger to appear, in long stockings and plumed hat, to blow a trumpet and unroll a proclamation. "Hear ye, hear ye," he would read. "The prisoners are forthwith freed!" And cries of "Hooray!" and "Yay!" would rise from the assembled throng.

But the minutes kept ticking away. It was 8:00. There had been no last-minute reprieve. The Gersons listened numbly to the radio until at last the smooth-voiced announcer intoned, "Convicted spies Julius and Ethel Rosenberg went to their deaths this evening in the electric chair at Sing Sing Prison."

"No!" Ellen cried. Her mother, across from her, huddled into herself, hands clutched together, head down. Her father reached out and held Ellen's hand. Ellen wanted to spin the dial away from the awful words that kept flowing, relentless as an ocean wave, from the radio. Instead she drew closer, rapt in morbid fascination.

"Thirty-five year old Julius Rosenberg was first to meet his maker, entering the brightly lit death chamber with halting steps. The first shock of two thousand volts was applied to his body at 8:04 P.M. After two additional shocks, he was declared dead at 8:06." The announcer's voice broke off and a new voice urged listeners to buy Wonder Bread, to "help build strong bodies seven ways." Then the first announcer took over again.

"Now it was Ethel Rosenberg's turn. Just a few minutes after the removal of her husband's body, she entered the death chamber. She wore a dark green dress printed with white polka dots, and her hair was cut short to allow contact with an electrode. The petite, five-foot, one-hundred-pound Mrs. Rosenberg held out her hand to the prison matron and kissed her cheek. As the prison rabbi said the Fifteenth Psalm, the first of three shocks was delivered at 8:11 P.M. She was examined by doctors following the third shock and found to be still alive."

Still alive! Ellen thought, hoping against hope. But the announcer continued his flat-toned narrative. "Two successive applications of current followed, and Ethel Rosenberg's life officially ended at 8:16 P.M. . . ."

Ellen continued to sit near the radio. She felt nothing so much as an absence of feeling. Mostly she felt tired, very tired. The patter that kept pouring from the set seemed to come from a long way off. The announcer's words which, just moments before, had cut through the air, sharp as knife blades, now sounded muffled.

"We take you now to our reporter in Union Square, where supporters of the Rosenbergs have kept up an all-day vigil. For their reactions . . ." Through the haze of words, Ellen heard singing. "Go down, Moses, way down in Egypt land . . ." When was it— two, three months ago that she had walked through New York City's streets, singing that same song and feeling so strong and powerful? Now she felt drained of every ounce of strength. Though the air was hot, dense, and humid, she began to shiver.

She stood and walked shakily to the front door, pulled it open, and sat down on the front step. Mikey followed her out and sat beside her. He pointed to the enormous ball of the sun, balanced on the horizon like a bloody tear. "Ellen made the sky red," he said, his face lit pink in its reflection.

Ellen shook her head, remembering a time, not very long ago, when he almost made her believe she *had* made the sky red. "No I didn't, Mikey. I'm just an ordinary person who can't do much of anything."

She rested her chin on her knees and stared, unseeing, at the sky. The screen door creaked open. Her mother touched her shoulder. "Judy's on the phone," she said. "She wants to know when you're coming over."

"Oh!" Ellen gave a start. The party. She touched a hand to her head and felt the masses of pincurls. "Tell her I'll be right over."

Ellen stood up and walked inside, pulling bobby pins from her hair on her way. She went into the bathroom and looked into the mirror. An explosion of curls ringed a pale face that she barely recognized as her own. Her reflection faded, obscured by a more powerful image. She saw Julius Rosenberg being escorted to the chair, solemn and dignified, between two guards. She saw him being strapped down, the wires that carried the electricity attached to his skin. She saw him being blindfolded. And then she saw a hand pull a giant switch. His body lurched upward, restrained only by the thick leather straps. His curly hair stood straight out from his scalp in a comic-strip depiction of fright, and then—oh, horror!—she saw a puff of smoke rise directly from the top of his head. The hand released the switch; his body slumped back. Dead.

Ellen replayed the scene, this time with Ethel Rosenberg in the title role. She walked toward the chair, so stately she might have been approaching a throne. Ellen saw her wipe a tear from the cheek of one of her female guards. She sat, modestly adjusting the hem of her polka-dot dress to cover her knees. She saw the hand, the switch, the straps, the wires, the blindfold, the rigid body, the puff of smoke. The death.

Ellen's eyes, still ringed with black liner, stared back at her through the awful images. The party, she thought. I have to get to the party. She picked up her brush and looked helplessly at her pin-curled head. It was no good. Her stomach contracted convulsively. Dropping the brush, she bent over and vomited into the toilet bowl again and again, until she retched from the depths of her empty stomach.

At last, straightening up, she swished some water and a dab of toothpaste around in her mouth to rid it of its vile taste. Then she stumbled into her room. She lay down on her bed. Just for a moment, she told herself. I have to get to the party.

But the images were re-forming before her eyes. A hand, a switch, a puff of smoke. She squeezed her eyes shut, but the pictures invaded her sealed lids. From far away she heard a telephone ring, muffled voices, her name. But she couldn't move. The one picture she kept seeing over and over and over, until tears spilled out and coursed down her cheeks, was of a small hand, tugging at the hem of a green polka-dot skirt. She turned her face into the pillow and sobbed. She never went to the party.

eleven

*E*llen woke on Saturday with a bad taste in her mouth and an unfocused, heavy feeling. She looked at the sky through her parted curtains. It was already an opaque white. The day was going to be as hot as yesterday.

Yesterday. Now it all came back. The Rosenbergs were dead.

She made her way to the bathroom, where she spent a long time brushing her teeth, trying to blot out the taste in her mouth with Ipana. When she raised her eyes to the mirror at last, she pulled back in confusion. Both cheeks were streaked with vertical black lines, seeming to announce her grief.

Silly, she told herself. The streaks were nothing more than a combination of tears and eye makeup. She soaped her hands well and rubbed the lather onto her cheeks, then rinsed her face clean. Now, when she looked into the mirror, the black lines were gone. No one need know her feelings—unless she wanted them to.

She tested a smile in front of the mirror and wondered, in spite of herself, how the party had been. Well, she thought, why should I be so upset? After all, people die every day, in all sorts of ways—car accidents, lightning, floods. I never knew the Rosenbergs. The fact that they were alive yesterday, but not today, isn't going to change my life. I can just go on doing the same things I did before. Can't I?

She went into the kitchen, where Mikey and Mrs. Gerson were having a breakfast of sorts together. Mikey, in his high chair, gripped a spoon with one hand and fed himself Cheerios. He used his other hand like a shovel, scooping up spilled Cheerios and dropping them into his mouth. He gave Ellen a big grin. Two soggy Cheerios dropped onto his chin.

"Hi, Hon," her mother said. She was taking quick little swallows of coffee from a steaming cup. Between sips she moved the radio dial. Every station seemed to have nothing but music. Muttering with impatience, Mrs. Gerson shut the set off. "I'm going to the shopping center for a newspaper," she said. "Want to come?"

What was her mother going to learn from a newspaper that she didn't already know? Ellen thought with annoyance. But she was used to her parents' insatiable craving for *news*. No matter what, they had to have a paper. Maybe things didn't seem quite real to them until they saw them in print.

Ellen shook her head. "No, I'll stay with Mikey." But Mikey was already out of his chair and following his mother to the door, always ready for a ride.

Ellen felt a sudden panic at the idea of being alone. "Where's Daddy?" she asked.

"He's still in bed. He must have been on the phone until two or three last night," Mrs. Gerson said. "Might as well let him sleep as late as he can."

Ellen nodded, glad that someone else was in the house. After her mother and Mikey left, she realized she was hungry. Her growling stomach was insistent. The box of Cheerios was still on the table; she poured some into a bowl for herself, added some milk, and started to eat.

A familiar shape flicked past the kitchen windows, followed by Judy's knock. Ellen didn't feel ready to face her. How was she going to explain her absence last night? But there was no way out. She opened the door.

"Hey, El. You okay? Your mom said you was sick."

Judy's concern made tears spring unexpectedly to Ellen's eyes. Who *can* I trust, if I can't trust Judy? she thought. Impulsively she decided to tell Judy the truth. "I . . . I wasn't really sick. I mean, I was throwing up. But that was because I was upset. About the Rosenbergs. The way they got killed. In the electric chair and all." There. She had said it.

"Poor El," Judy said. "What a softy. But you shoulda come to the party. We would have cheered you up. And I bet you would have got Donny's clue."

"Clue? What do you mean?" Ellen asked.

"It was so funny," Judy said. "We were playing charades and Don Butowski's category was current events. I can't do it anywheres near as good as he did, but it was something like this." Judy crossed her eyes and went rigid, while her body vibrated in place. "Get it? Those commie spies you was talking about. The ones got burned last night. *Current* events. You know, like in an electric current. Nobody guessed what Donny was doing. But if you was there, I bet you'da known right off."

Ellen, mute with horror, stared at Judy. "You mean," she said at last, "it was a joke? Two people being electrocuted?"

"Well, yeah. Kinda sick, I know," Judy admitted. "But it was funny—Donny's joke, I mean. And it's like John Ballantine said, 'The only good commie's a dead commie.' Now there's two less to worry about. Do ya see?"

As Judy spoke, Ellen felt as though her blood were draining from her body. She had to sit down. "Yes," she said. She put a hand to her head. "Look, I can't talk now," Ellen said. Leaving Judy at the front door, she turned and walked into her bedroom.

She had heard Judy's words, Ellen realized, without much surprise. This was Judy—direct, open, but certainly not sentimental. She had never pretended to be different. It was Ellen who had pretended, Ellen who had chosen Judy as her model. So now the disgust, the revulsion she felt was not toward Judy, but toward herself.

She sat on her bed, feeling overwhelmed. So how do you make the right choices? she thought. What about the Rosenbergs? Did they choose to die? To abandon their children? Ellen thought of the crumpled picture she still kept between the pages of her book. She felt a stab of anger at Julius and Ethel Rosenberg for making orphans of their own sons. Maybe they didn't choose death directly, she conceded. But they did choose to be communists, didn't they? And wasn't their communism one of the reasons they were killed?

What about her parents? If they were arrested tomorrow and given a choice of abandoning communism or abandoning their children, which would they choose? Ellen was all too sure she knew the answer. It wasn't comforting.

What about Judy? Did she have a hard time making choices? Ellen could imagine Judy mulling over whether to paint her nails Passionate Peach or Persian Melon. But anything more serious . . . well . . . Ellen smiled.

I like Judy, she thought. But I don't want to *be* like her. The realization was a hard one for Ellen to accept. The nearness of Judy in her life these last couple of months had worked like a magic charm, bringing her wealth beyond measure—acceptance, even popularity. Just thinking about turning away from Judy gave Ellen a sense of loss, a vague emptiness.

So what do I do now? Ellen thought. A picture of Sue's dark head, bent under the taunts of her classmates, swam before her eyes.

I know one thing, she thought. I don't want to be a person who abandons her friends—*or* one who laughs while someone dies.

When Ellen and Judy met on Monday morning for their walk to the bus stop, Ellen felt protective of her friend. For the first time, she felt older than Judy, aware of a harsh world outside that Judy might never know. She linked her arm through Judy's, and they walked in step to the bus stop.

Mr. Gleason had just collected the science textbooks when the air raid siren sounded.

"Do you believe this?" Kevin Connolly grumbled beside her. "Five more days till the end of school and they're still making us go through this dumb act."

"Yeah. Duck and cover, duck and cover," another boy mimicked in Mr. Slavin's high-pitched voice.

The grumbling continued, but everyone stood, pushing back the chairs with the nerve-grating screech of metal against tile, and filed into the hall.

Tucked into her compact hump along the wall, Ellen held her knees tightly as the siren petered out and the recorded roar of a jet boomed overhead. Then it was Mr. Slavin's turn. "Being prepared is a three-hundred-sixty-five-days-a-year job. Just because summer vacation is approaching . . ."

Ellen had stoppered her ears to muffle Mr. Slavin's words. Though she braced herself against the wall, she began shivering with tension. Images of death crowded in on her—a massive wooden chair draped with electric wires, eerily lit tunnels filled with gun-carrying soldiers, bombs hurtling toward Earth from soaring airplanes. Suddenly she knew why these air raid drills were so terrible. Instead of saving lives, they made bombing, war, killing seem possible. And those things should be impossible. Impossible.

She had to do something. She couldn't continue to cower here in the body-lined corridor. The bones in her knees cracked as she raised herself from her crouch and stood up. Kevin Connolly glanced at her across the top of his folded arms. "Hey, Ellen, get down," he hissed. "Someone's coming."

"No, I can't," she said. She could hear footsteps approaching, and she turned her head quickly to see who was coming. Mr. Mitchell. Oh, no, she thought. Her right knee began to jiggle. Of all people. Why did it have to be him?

As he closed the gap between them, it took all of Ellen's will not to fold herself into the crouch position again.

Mr. Mitchell touched her shoulder lightly. "Are you all right, Ellen?" he asked in the soft, gravelly voice she liked so much. She wished her voice would come out low and gravelly too, but instead it piped out a frightened squeak.

"Yes." She swallowed. "But I'm not going to duck and cover anymore. It's . . . it's dumb." That wasn't what she meant to say. She wanted to tell him, calmly and reasonably, that air raid drills were wrong, that they only increased the risk of war. But it was hard enough just to stand there, both knees jiggling uncontrollably now, without buckling.

Mr. Mitchell backed off slightly. "Come on, Ellen. Why make trouble for yourself? School's almost over. Just bend down a little, okay? I'll say you had cramps."

Ellen felt herself blush. "I'm sorry, Mr. Mitchell," she said. "I can't."

"So you're deliberately disobeying Mr. Slavin's orders?" he asked.

Ellen could feel the eyes of other students peeking at her. Not trusting her voice, she turned to Mr. Mitchell and nodded.

"You know I'm going to have to report you," he said, and Ellen nodded again.

He shook his head, turned, and walked away. His head was bent and his footsteps sounded hesitant as they receded down the hall. Ellen felt a rush of pity for him. She had an urge to call out, "Wait! I'm sorry. I didn't mean it!" But she knew she had made her choice. There was no going back.

As Mr. Mitchell disappeared around the corner, she envisioned the one thing she'd thought she most wanted disappearing with him—the chance to be an ordinary American girl. Miss Fairmore Hills Junior High. The image shimmered before her. Her eyes filled with tears.

Did it really matter all that much? she wondered. She wished she could answer no—and mean it. It did matter. Not enough, though. Not enough to make her bend her knees.